IN THE COUN

BY

C.S ANDERSON

A Black Irish Novel

Alucard Press 2014

CHAPTER ONE

Time has no meaning to the dead or to those who sleep. Dreams that seem to go on forever are actually over in heartbeats. Time flows around the dreamer like a river flows around a stone in its path.

I have been that stone.

I awaken to the cawing of a raven.

As I awaken I only know that this place is not the place that I fell into my slumber. I do not remember what that place was but I somehow know that I am no longer in it.

Such memories dangle just out of my reach. I can feel them there but I can't touch them. A sly voice in the deeper shadows of my mind whispers that just maybe that is for the best.

"For the best." The raven croaks.

I can focus my eyes now and I see that I am sitting at a long bar, nicked up and covered in cigarette burns. The raven stares down at me from its cage behind and above the bar.

I am not alone.

An old man is polishing glasses with his back to me behind the bar humming a tune that it seems I used to know, forgotten along with everything else right now.

"For the best." The raven croaks again.

It is already starting to get on my damn nerves.

I take a long look around the place, as far as I can tell, me and the old man have the place to ourselves.

Well, and the raven too, I suppose.

Dim greyish light filters in through the dirty windows. There is an older than dirt pool table behind me and some torn up booths by the window. The place is a dive but that's ok by me.

I have always liked drinking in dives.

"Drinking in dives." The damn bird croaks again.

There is now a drink in front of me, would have sworn that there hadn't been one there just a moment ago and the old man is still polishing glasses behind the bar.

"Where am I?" I ask out loud, my voice startles me. It is the voice of a stranger and I have no memory of hearing it before.

"Welcome to my tavern friend." The old man says as he turns around to face me.

I somehow know who he is at once.

You would think that The Devil would be more fearsome in appearance. He stands there smiling at me, just another old Irish Codger. The kind that has poured me a drink in many a dumps such as this. Nose like a potato, washed out green eyes and bad teeth.

"Welcome." Croaks the raven.

"So am I dead then? Is this hell?" I ask him quietly as I pick up my drink.

"Well, boyo, that is actually the matter of no little debate just now, it is indeed. To answer the second question, no this isn't hell, just a little place I like to putter around in from time to time." He tells me with a small shrug and a nonchalant wave of his wrinkled hand.

The whiskey in the glass is excellent. I can honestly say that is the best whiskey I can ever remember having. I tell the old man that and we both have a little chuckle over that.

The raven watches us with his beady eyes as if puzzled somehow by the laughter. Likely not a sound it hears all that often.

"You are a piece of work lad that you are indeed. Brace yourself, this is going to sting a bit." He warns me.

"What is?" I barely have enough time to ask the question before his hand flashes out and slaps me hard across the face.

"Remember." Croaks the raven.

And I do.

Every fucking thing!

It all crashes over me like a dark massive wave trying its level best to drown me. Images, sensations, emotions all of it comes flooding back into my mind. All of it, the faces of those I served up to my vampire Master before becoming a Gun and all those I have killed while doing my penance, flashing before my eyes. All my battles, all my struggles.

And above all else, Keela.

After the wave passes, I pull myself back up off of the dirty floor and struggle back onto my stool.

"Well I'll be damned." I muttered.

"With any luck." The old man says with a huge grin.

I sip my whiskey and take a moment to try to put all of the memories into a semblance of context. It isn't easy, but slowly I start putting the pieces together.

Brain pushed the detonator just as I dove under the Humvee, the very last thing I remember is the thunder of the blast.

"So, am I dead then?" I ask again.

"By all rights you should be. Hells man that was a lot of plastic explosives! The Humvee shot up a few dozen feet and the fireball consumed everything leaving nothing but a blackened crater." The old guy shakes his head ruefully as he tops off our glasses.

"Not dead." The raven croaks.

The old man gives the bird a very hard stare and it retreats to the furthest corner of the cage and falls silent.

"Hush Twilla." He hisses at it.

"You used dark magic instinctively and vanished into the shadow under the Humvee so you didn't fry like the vampire and his pretty little sword did. Not having so much as one fucking clue about what you were doing, you got lost in the shadows for a time. You ended up sleeping on The Morrigan's throne, it took me a very long time to find you lad."

Didn't much like the sound of that, why had he been looking for little old me?

"Relax, I half own your soul already and I am not truly in a hurry to collect. You, well you intrigue me. Such an odd mix of magics, you are. Such an interesting mix of violence and redemption, you are quite entertaining in your own way. To paraphrase a quote from a popular movie, the world is more interesting with you in it."

Entertaining, well I have definitely been called worse.

"So send me back then and I will continue to entertain you." I tell him off hand, I know it is bound to be way more complicated than that.

He stares at me for a very long moment without blinking, his lined face unreadable. After a moment he sighs and pours us each another measure of the whiskey.

"It is of course a bit more complicated than that. Everything has a price lad, you know that."

"So what's the price tag then? You say you aren't after my soul so what the hell, pardon the expression, do you want?" I demand. Keela fills my thoughts, I can't believe that I forgot her so completely when she is all I can think about now. Her and the child she bears.

"Time passes." The raven croaks above us.

"That is does, lad. It passes differently in different realms but passes it does no matter where you find yourself."

It hits me then what he is getting at.

How long was I lost in the shadows? Will I be like Rip Van Winkle and awake to find all I care about long dead and gone? A cold knot forms in my stomach as Keela's face flashes through my eyes.

"Dead and gone." The raven croaks.

The fucking thing is starting to get on my last damn nerves.

"Hush Twilla." The old man shushes the bird with a dismissive wave of his hands.

"Let us get down to business then shall we?" He asks me with an unpleasant smile.

Like the old saying goes boys and girls,

The Devil is in the details.

CHAPTER TWO

He poured us each another drink and we walked over to an empty dusty booth and sat down. The windows were so filthy that I couldn't see a damn thing out of them.

All things considered, I doubt I was missing much of a view.

"All right then first things first, you want to know how long you have been gone? And then you will want to know how I will send you back, am I correct?" His voice was on the surface warm but it had a cold sly undercurrent to it.

I gave him a nod and took a sip of my whiskey.

"Well boyo, for today only I am running a two for one special. The answer to the first question will cost you but the answer for the second question is free of charge."

"And let me guess, if I order before midnight you throw in a set of steak knives for free?"

Yeah, I am still a raging smart ass. Nice to know that some things never change.

The smile he flashes at me never touches his eyes.

"Keep that sense of humor my friend. You are going to need it soon enough. No, no steak knives, I am afraid but that does give me an idea. An idea that we will revisit in just a bit."

It doesn't really matter what the price tag is, I think both of us at the table know that. Whatever he asks for we both know that I will be willing to pay. I have to get back to the world I left.

"Enough foreplay old man, what the fuck do you want?"

I don't work and play well with others.

"Very well then my impatient young friend. Straight to business it is. The cost of the answer to the first question will be one of your eyes. You can even pick which one." He tells me calmly.

Leaning back in my part of the booth, I give him a long hard stare. He stares back completely unimpressed.

"Seriously?"

He gives me a mischievous look and raises his glass in a mocking toast.

"No man, I am just fucking with you. You don't get to pick it has to be the left one."

"What the fuck do you want with my left eye?"

"That would be my business lad. It is a straight up trade. A simple business really. You give me your left eye, I not only tell you how long you have been gone from the world but I help you find your way home. Easy peasy lemon squeezy."

Honestly not sure which bothered me more the fact that he wanted my left eye or he just totally said, "Easy peasy lemon squeezy."

Maybe I was dead, maybe this was hell and he was just toying with me before tossing me into some firey pit or whatever. Or maybe I somehow lived through the explosion and all this was a morphine dream, as I lay dying in Harborview's burn unit. Didn't really matter, one way or the other I needed to end this and go see Keela, if only in whatever dream this might be.

"Done." I told him through gritted teeth.

His smile is truly awful.

The raven caws loudly behind us and distracted for a moment, I turn towards the sound.

Pain explodes on the left side of my face as his wrinkled hand whips in and tears my eye out.

"Oh don't be such a pussy. Here you can have one of mine you big baby!" He scoffs at me.

He pulls out his own left eye and before I can even react, he plunges it into the empty socket he just created. Then he calmly pops my eye into his face.

A scream tries to rise in my throat as his eye burns with a terrible icy coldness. I choke it back down and pound my fist on the table until the sensation finally passes, because I just don't want to give the bastard the fucking satisfaction of hearing me scream.

"That likely stung a bit lad, have some more whiskey."

"How..long..have..I…been…gone?" I spit the words out one at a time.

"Ten long years, bitch isn't it?" He tells me as he refills first my glass and then his own.

It hits me like a fist. Ten fucking years. So much time passing, my child almost half way to adulthood. Keela, God knows ten years is a long time to be alone. Brain, either a legendary Gun by now or dead. The Order either a corrupted mockery of itself or the thin line between the world of humans and the world of vampires.

"Send me back." I ask him as I drain my glass.

"Back." Croaks the raven in its cage.

"That would be the general idea lad. Just so we are clear, I can see what you will be up to now that you carry my eye with you. Once you return I will have no influence over events but I am hoping for a good show." He flashes me a predatory grin.

"I will try not to disappoint you, you fuck. What now? Do I click my damn heels three times and say that there is no mother fucking place like home or what?"

He regards me with a patient and mocking smile that has more than a little cruelty in it. The form he is wearing flickers just a bit and suddenly that smile is full of wickedly sharp looking teeth.

"Few more things to address first lad, slow down. You've been gone ten years, a few minutes isn't going to matter much in the scheme of things."

He snaps his fingers and the raven is suddenly no longer in the hanging cage, it is in the middle of the table between us.

The bird shimmers for an instant and then dissolves into a splotch of a dark inky looking gel that oozes across the table and up my arm. It stings like hell as it soaks in and disappears.

Well, not quite disappears.

It leaves behind a small tattoo on my left wrist, the image is a stylized silhouette of a raven. The tattoo is crude compared to the one that was placed on my chest by the Fey tattoo artist Rhune and it has a sense of wrongness about it.

"Not quite steak knives lad, but a parting gift just the same." The old bastard sounds very pleased with himself.

That should probably worry me more than it does.

No room for that particular worry in my thoughts, Keela is all I can think about, her and our child. I have to know what has become of them. Brain had promised to look after them but I had no way of knowing if he was even still alive to do so.

Ten years is a very long time, our business being what it is, a lot of Guns don't last anywhere near that long.

Death is basically our retirement program.

"Send me back." I tell him grimly.

He leans back and gives me a long considering look, his arms crossed over is chest. After a few seconds he sighs deeply and gives me a slight nod.

"Very well then lad. You being what you are and the world being what it is we will likely meet again. When we do, there will be less courtesy and negotiation involved than this time. You will remember this meeting when you return to your world, but I have placed a compulsion on you not to speak of it to anyone. Tell them any story you like about where you have been, but leave my name out of it."

He snaps his fingers and a trap door appears on the floor next to the booth.

"Open it. Then drop through and you will be back in your world. Do not try the traveling through shadows bit again, you suck at it. Go forth now and let the games begin…"

And then he is gone.

I stand up and stare down at the trap door, I'm alone in the silent bar. Picking up my glass of whiskey, I finish it and then fling it against the far wall of the bar where it shatters.

Reaching down I grab the iron ring set into the door and pull it open. I stare down into the deep darkness that lay beneath the door but there is nothing to see.

Sometimes the only way to see if the stove is hot, is to touch it.

I close my eyes and say a quick prayer, even though that seems vastly inappropriate in this particular place and time.

And then I drop through.

CHAPTER THREE

There is one horrible moment of wrenching pain and nausea and then another moment of icy numbness as I fall through the doorway before I hit the ground with a jarring thud.

It is late afternoon, maybe three hours until darkfall. I am not sure but I think I am somewhere in the Belltown neighborhood. Not a soul is in sight, which is more than weird because normally this part of the city is bustling all day and night. Most of the buildings windows are boarded up and the few cars parked are burned out wrecks. I look up and the sky looks, odd. There is a dark barely perceptible oily looking shimmer to it. Already getting that old Scooby Doo "Ruh Roh" feeling.

The tattoo the old fuck gave me gives a spasm of pain that drives me to my knees and as I watch the ink oozes down my arm and begins to slither away from me across the rubble filled sidewalk. When it is about twenty feet away it stops and begins to ooze upward congealing into a small human sized shape.

I blink my eyes and there is a scrawny punk rock looking chick about five foot nothing grinning back at me. Her skin is paper white and her hair is short spikes of the deepest black I have ever seen. She is wearing mostly leather and chains and her black boots have wicked looking metal points on the toes.

"I'm not a fucking bird!" She yells and starts doing cartwheels and hand springs all over the damn place.

She pirouettes up to me and with a sly grin ankle sweeps me onto my ass. In one smooth move she is straddling me and staring intently down at me.

"Thank you thank you thank you! I am called Twilla and my Master bids me to serve you in what is to come!" She chirps at me with a manic look on her face.

I roll her off of me and she runs around in erratic circles cackling like a mad witch.

"Not a bird! Not a bird! Not a bird!" She chortles gleefully in an unending litany as she starts doing jumping jacks.

Well, this sucks. He sent me back with a being that was like a hyper active child on crack. I stand up wondering how the hell things could get worse.

And then, well of course I find the fuck out.

Three Dark Adepts step out of the shadows and surround us.

One is tall and thin with a spikey mane of blonde hair, one is short and squat and looks like he chews on razor blades to unwind and the third is the scariest of them all.

He looks so damn normal.

Average weight, average height, average build, average attractiveness. So average that he was almost invisible.

Bland to the point of the same. Evil boiled off the skin of his being like heat waves off of an Arizona highway.

"What have we here? Please state your designations and show us your brands." He asks in a bored tone.

Twilla rolls her oddly colored eyes that seem to shift in color each time I look at them.

"Crap these bozos get on my nerves! Boss allows them a tiny bit of power so that they can be his agents on this dirt pile and they think they are fucking demons! Give me a break!" She scoffs as she pats me softly on the back.

Well I just so happen to not have either a designation or a brand, so things are likely to get a little complicated up in here in a damn hurry.

Then I remember that I am outnumbered and have no weapons on me.

They all do, unusually enough. The Dark Adepts I have encountered didn't carry weapons but this little party seems to have missed that memo because each of them has a gun on their hip. It gives me a bit of hope that none of them have been smart enough to draw one yet.

You know that old saying live and learn? There also exists a direct opposite.

"Howdy boys!" Twilla shouts as she bounces back over to where they stand.

Bad move. They all draw their guns and point them at her. The bland one is also forming a curse in his left hand to fling.

"Group hug!" She giggles as she wraps her arms around all of them while pulling them to her.

"Duck and cover Black Irish!"

I take her warning at face value and dive away to my left just before she explodes.

Yeah, she exploded.

As in, boom!

Like a hand grenade, she goes off splattering our dark robed friends into kibbles and bits in all directions. A blood soaked gun skitters by me and I snatch it up and I cannot begin to tell you how good it feels to have one in my hand again.

Feels like coming home.

I stand there with the gun in my hand looking for more trouble but it seems my little friend has taken care of things pretty thoroughly. As I watch rivulets of black ooze begin to flow back into the epicenter of the blast once again congealing into a humanoid shape.

"And she's back!" She announces while jumping up and down for no apparent reason.

"Nice trick you've got there. Thanks for the help but you can run along back to your boss now." I tell her as I stuff the gun into my waistband.

"Sorry pal, you are stuck with me. Where you go I go. Only way to get rid of me is to get yourself killed. I'd appreciate it if you held off on that for a while though, the fun is really just starting!" She tells me with a lurid wink.

Perfect.

"Oh, don't make such a face Black Irish! I will grow on you, I can as you have just seen, be very useful, plus I know things." She stage whispers the last sentence at me.

We are burning daylight here, I need to figure out what the hell is going on and work out how I am going to find Keela and Brain. I don't even know if either of them is even still alive but I push that thought away. For now I will operate on the assumption that they are.

"What sort of things?" I ask her as calmly as I can.

She gives me a pouty face and turns her back on me.

"If you want to know you have to say, pretty please with sugar on top." She tells me petulantly.

I consider my options. They all suck.

If she can explode and reform like she just did, I doubt my threatening to shoot her is going to sway her much.

"Pretty please?" I ask her through gritted teeth.

"With sugar on top." She reminds me in a little girl's voice that makes me want to reconsider trying to shoot her.

"With fucking sugar on top. Talk to me Twilla."

Her face lights up in a huge smile and she skips cheerfully over to me. She sits down on the ground and pats the ground next to her. Her fingernails are black and I doubt if it is nail polish, they also look sharp.

"Sit down then you big galoot and let me give you the 411!" She giggles at me.

Not having a clue what the hell else to do, I sigh and sit my ass down next to her.

CHAPTER FOUR

"Once upon a time…." She begins, her voice is solemn but there is a mocking grin on her face.

My patience is gone, I snap my hand out and grab the front of her shirt and give her a hard shake.

"Cut the bullshit imp, tell me what happened and make it the damn Reader's Digest version because it will be dark soon and I have a lot to do before then."

Her eyes flash red for a split second and for that same instant her face is a feral mask of rage. The moment passes and she gives me a small nod so I let her go. She scoots back a little placing herself just out of my reach. Giving me a slightly wounded look she continues with her story.

"After you took your little stroll into the shadows, things went south for humans around here pretty fast. Both your own Order and The Vampire Council were fractured and while they were busy cleaning house a rouge element of elder vamps conspired with a splinter group of Dark Adepts to pull off a coup. With the new power structure of The Council vampires came out of the shadows and openly attacked the humans of this city. The city fell in days as the Dark Adepts sealed the city behind a barrier spell so that no help could come. That oily shimmer you noticed in the sky is that barrier spell. Your Order in other territories convinced the government that what was going on in the city was a lethal and highly contagious biological outbreak that had to be contained and that the barrier was advanced technology in the hands of unknown terrorist's. Seattle and everything within thirty miles of it is now quarantined with troops stationed to make sure it stays that way. It has been that way for almost nine years now." She tells me all this like she is talking about getting her nails done.

"Where are all the people?" I ask her quietly, my mind reeling at what she is telling me. I want to think that she is lying but her words have the ring of truth to them.

"Tens of thousands died in the early days, until the vamps figured out that it didn't make sense to wipe out their food supply. Humans are now mostly confined to camps where they are branded as blood slaves to different vampire elders. They are kept alive to continue supplying blood for as long as possible and encouraged to breed. Human servants and Dark Adepts run the show during the day. A few branded humans are designated as dayslaves to run errands for various vamps. The guys I splattered would have killed you for being undesignated and unbranded. The only unbranded humans now are the underground resistance. They call themselves The Human Resistance Organization." She continues in the same bored tone.

I held up my hand to buy a moment to process all that she had told me. It was grim news, my order had failed and the city had fallen to the things we had taken vows to defend it against. The only glimmer of good news was that there was a resistance, which was definitely a party I needed to crash.

"Cheer up Black Irish, it could be worse." She told me with a wicked grin.

"How?" The moment I asked the question I knew I was going to regret asking it.

"It could be raining."

Of course the moment she said that, a low rumble of thunder sounded off in the distance and a light rain began to fall.

"Oops." She giggled and I knew that this was not going to be the beginning of a beautiful friendship.

"How do we contact the resistance?" I asked her as I stood up. We need to move and sort things out as we go.

"By tossing your gun away, and then both of you putting your hands on top of your heads and turning around really fucking slow." A deep voice informs me from behind us.

That is followed by the sound of about eight guns having their safeties clicked off.

Crap.

I toss the gun away and follow the rest of the spiel, turning around like the man said, really fucking slow.

"Don't blow anybody up." I hiss at Twilla who sighs dramatically and also puts her hands on her head.

Eight scruffy looking guys have spread out and are pointing a motley collection of weapons at us. One has an ancient looking sawed off shotgun with the splintered stock wrapped in grimy duct tape and the guy next to him has an old Russian bolt action army rifle that is far older than he is. They all look like they have been living hardscrabble for a long while now.

"They are here, just like the little freak said they would be." The guy with the shotgun says in a gruff voice.

"Shut up Brett." The guy with the bolt action says in a bored tone, like he tells Brett to shut up several times a day. He is a medium sized guy with long graying hair pulled back in a ponytail and what looks like a knife scar on his right cheek.

"Who are you people?" He asks quietly giving us a long hard stare.

"My name is Joe, this is Twilla. We aren't looking for any trouble. Can we dial it down a couple of notches and maybe lower some guns?" I ask politely.

Politeness is called for sometimes, especially times when lots of people, who look like they know how to use them, have guns pointed at you and when you lack one yourself.

He looks us both over carefully, especially Twilla who is giving him a flirty smile. The guy is human so all he can tell is that there is something off about her. An adept or a trained Gun would be able to tell that she is an imp.

I really don't want to try and explain to the guy why I am traveling with a lesser demon who basically exists to spread mischief and trouble.

Finally he nods and gestures at his crew to lower their weapons. One by one they all do with our buddy Brett being the last one to do so.

"My name is Jones. We have orders to collect you and bring you back for questioning. Night is coming so we aren't going to debate anything I am about to tell you. First, you don't get your gun back just yet, we will be hanging onto that for you for now. Second you both will be blindfolded until we get to where we are going." His tone is flat and like he said, does not invite spirited debate.

"And if that doesn't work for us?" Twilla asks him cheerfully as she lowers her arms.

"Shut up Twilla, it works for us." I tell Jones and he gives me a small smile.

"Good let's move."

Two guys take out black cloth bags and put them over our heads. The same two start to lead us away to wherever we are going.

"Ok you two don't do anything stupid and we will be where we need to be in an hour or so. Move out people." Jones barks out the order like he is used to doing so.

"Yeah come on you fucks we are off to see the wizard." Brett says in a snide tone from somewhere to my left.

"Shut up Brett." Jones tells him in the same bored tone as before just with slightly more of an edge to it.

Off to see the wizard.

I can only pray that that means what I hope it does.

CHAPTER FIVE

We walk through the light rain for what has to be at least an hour, the guy guiding me by the elbow is good at it and it is clear that he has done this before. My marks tingle slightly so I know Twilla is still with us. She has been quiet which should probably worry me.

I spend the time of the walk digesting all that the imp told me before we were so rudely interrupted. Assuming any and all of it is true, things are pretty damn grim.

Ten fucking years.

The city has fallen, and that is on us in The Order. It was our duty to protect this city and it would appear that we have drastically failed. This cuts me deeply, for all my various insubordinate actions and sarcastic responses to dumb orders, I served my Order to the best of my ability, always. The Order was the framework of my existence and to know that at least here in this city it no longer exists, is bitter medicine.

Keela and my child.

More bitter medicine to swallow.

She thinks I am dead, have been dead for years now. Has she moved on? Is there someone else? The thought of it is a sick weight in my gut, not that I could blame her. The wheel of my thoughts keep coming back to a basic point.

Ten fucking years.

My child, boy or girl now halfway to adulthood. No first words or first steps or first any damn thing for me to have as memories. We will be strangers to one another assuming that I can even find them. So much time lost, so much lost in general.

Fuck it, enough whining introspection. It is what it is. Take it in steps, find them and see what is what and what comes next. Our buddy Brett mentioned someone called "The Wizard."

Back in the day I knew a man who claimed that as one of his names. I called him Brain and I trained him to be a Gun like me. He swore an oath to me before blowing me and the ancient vamp to hell that he would watch out for Keela and the baby.

If these guys are taking me to who I hope that they are, I will be that much closer to getting the answers I seek.

Whether I like those answers or not.

The bag over my head isn't as effective as our new pals likely think it is. My left eye, the one the old man swapped with me can see right through it but, I let the man leading me think that I need him to do so. The view isn't pretty, more rubble and burned out cars and buildings. The sun is going down and I find myself hoping that we are getting close to wherever we are going. Things are going to get bad around here at darkfall.

I suspect that Twilla can see through her bag as well when I notice her sticking her tongue out at me. For the moment she is behaving herself and I can only pray that she will continue to do so.

The men around me are good, even Brett. They function as a well-trained squad. Constantly checking all possible angles, watching each other's backs while watching us constantly as well. All of them always keeping a watchful eye on the setting sun.

As the sun sets my hand aches for a gun. I feel like I have been dumped into a new game that there is no rule book for and a gun in my hand would make me a hell of a lot happier right now.

The gun I picked up after Twilla blew up our Dark Adept friends is now stuck in the waistband of this merry little group's leader. It is by far the best gun that is being carried right now and I want the damn thing back.

I want it back a hell of a lot more once the approaching night is filled with the not far away enough sound of howling dogs.

They sound really big.

They sound really hungry.

"Growlers." Brett mutters as the whole group begins to pick up the pace until we are running towards a boarded up derelict apartment building.

"Move it people." Jones says tersely as we all move through the shattered doorway.

The moment we are all inside Brett and two other men swing a heavy slab of steel plating over the remains of the door and moving with the speed of a lot of practice, they use chains and padlocks to secure it.

Whatever is making the howling noises is getting closer and it sounds like there is more than one. The sound is truly awful, like no dog or even wolf I have ever heard. I don't know what the hell a growler is and I am in no fucking hurry to find out.

We are most of the way down a long dark hallway before the sound of large angry whatever the hell they are, are slamming into the steel plating. Brett flinches at the sound and even Jones looks like he would really like to be somewhere else right now.

"Move it!" He repeats waving us toward an apartment door to our left as he covers our retreat with the gun he took from me. His face is grim but I don't see any fear in it.

Twilla shoots me a quick glance and I give her the slightest of nods telling her to keep on following these men.

We are through the apartment door in seconds and they lead us straight to a large walk in closet. One of the men pulls a large floor rug out of the way to reveal a trap door eerily like the one I dropped through to get my ass back home. He unlocks it with a key he had on a leather thong around his neck and one by one we all clamber down a ladder leading us down below street level. Jones is the last one down and he closes the trap door behind us.

They all break out flashlights and we move through the tunnel we dropped down into. I curl my fingers into a standard revelation glyph and I mutter the words that I have been taught. That slight magic flashes out and reveals that which was hidden. I see a glyph carved into a support beam and it tells me that this little underground passage was created by The Order. We splash through a few bad smelling puddles as we go.

The men leading us have all visibly chilled now that we are underground and presumably safe from whatever the hell a growler is and away from the immediate threat of vampires, since the sun is surely down by now.

Which means that the streets above us are now owned by the vampires and we need to hide.

In this world, in this time, all we humans are an endangered species.

We go through a steel door set into the wall of the tunnel into a large room that looks like it might have once served as a cafeteria. Jones gives the men leading us the nod and they pull the bags off our heads.

"What the fuck is a growler?" I ask as I make a show of blinking at the sudden light.

"A master vamp named Donatello raises them, mastiffs bred for size and viciousness and then fed a fun diet of human blood and flesh laced with tiny amounts of vampire blood. Think guard dogs on steroids with an instinctive hatred and hunger for humans. Packs of them roam the city, we have lost good people to them." Jones tells us flatly.

"I like puppies." Twilla says flippantly, the way she is baring her teeth makes me think she means as an appetizer more than a pet.

He gives her a long hard stare but then decides to ignore her and turns his attention to me.

"I would ask you where the hell you are from that you don't know what a growler is but I have the feeling that your answer is above my pay grade. Wait here for a bit, Brett here will get you some grub. Boss man will be joining us shortly and he can ask you those kind of questions."

Everyone sits down at the table as Brett hands out some MRE meals he pulls from a cabinet. Nobody is pointing any guns at us, but we aren't exactly free to leave either. The food tastes like crap but we all wolf it down anyway, there is little to no witty dinner time banter.

The glyph I saw tells me that The Order still exists, if only as the frame work of the resistance. The HRO using its old infrastructures and supplies to keep the fight going. If Brain is in charge he would have knowledge of places like this, even if the rest of The Order had crumbled. Any knowledge I have of supply depots, safe houses and what not is a decade out of date and therefore mostly fucking useless. The weapons these guys are carrying tells me that we are likely down to seeds and stems on supplies.

They knew we were coming, they had specifically been sent to meet us and bring us in. How was that possible? Who was 'the little freak' Brett had referred to? So many damn questions.

And not a lot of answers to be had so far.

A door opens in the back of the room and the man I used to call Brain limps in with an armed guard on either side of him. They have the look of Guns about them but they aren't old enough to be actual Guns.

We make eye contact and all hell breaks loose.

CHAPTER SIX

His face is more lined and gaunt than I remember and his hairline more receded, but it is him. Brain, the man I trained to become a Gun and the man who pushed the button on the bomb that took out an insane elder vamp and supposedly myself. He is leaning on a cane and moving stiffly and as I watch his eyes first widen in shock and then narrow in rage.

As he approaches me, men scatter out of his way, Brett moves a little slow so my old friend backhands him out of the way. He draws a sword from the cane and puts the tip a fraction of an inch from my throat.

"Whatever the fuck you are, you do yourself no favors by taking the form of my dead friend. You also do yourself no favors by coming to me with that, creature in tow. I highly fucking recommend you start explaining yourself now before my limited patience runs out." He hisses at me through clenched teeth.

"Dial it down trainee, hard as it is to believe, it is me." I tell him calmly looking him in the eye.

Brain has always walked a thin bloody line with his temper and I can see him struggling with it now. The dark rage filled part of him wants nothing more than to use the sword to tear my throat open and I watch him win the struggle not to do that.

He puts out a hand and snaps his fingers. Jones steps up carefully and places the gun he took from me into his hand.

"Password." He barks at me placing the barrel of the gun in the exact center of my forehead.

"Asshole." I tell him with a grim smile.

There is a moment of absolute silence and stillness in the room as we stand there like that.

"Close enough, brother. Close enough." He says in a shock filled whisper.

And then he faints.

I move fast and catch him on the way down and help him over to a nearby chair. Maybe a little too fast, Jones's eyes widen and he takes a step towards us, but I back him off with a hard look.

"Well that went well!" Twilla chirps to the room at large. She is leaning up against the far wall with an amused smile on her face, her arms crossed her chest. The look she gives me says that she will back whatever play I make here but given her choice she would cheerfully slaughter everyone in the room.

"Everyone but him and his friend out." Brain says weakly waving a hand towards the door. His people hesitate but they obey leaving us alone.

"Talk to me." He says looking up at me with eyes that are a hell of lot older than the last time I saw him. The lines on his face tell an unhappy story about how hard the ten years has been on him.

I sit down with him and give him a heavily edited version of the story, beginning by reminding him that he had theorized that due to what had been done to me by an ancient master vamp trying to create a vampire who could wield magic, I had gained the ability to travel through shadows like a Dark Adept. I explained that I had become lost in those shadows and that in them I had encountered the imp and that together we had found our way out.

"Your turn, Brain. What the fuck happened?"

Good thing for Twilla his story more or less matched the version she had given me about the fall of Seattle. He told it with a little more emotion than she had but the basic facts matched up. She gives me a bored I told you so shrug, as I listen.

"Keela and the baby." I say quietly after we had sat silently for a few moments.

"Both alive Joe, both here. Congratulations it's a boy by the way. His name is Tumaini, he is, well, what he is makes for a long story. He for lack of a better term is a clairvoyant. He told us that someone important to the resistance would be showing up right when and where we found you. He left out that it would be his own father, his visions tend to run like that. Nuggets of intel lacking details."

So my boy was the 'little freak' Brett had referred to.

Interesting.

He and I would be discussing that later.

At length.

The door flies open and Keela storms in and the sight of her nearly stops my damn heart. Too much has been happening for me to even wonder what this moment would be like, she is so beautiful that it is almost physically painful to look at her. I stand up and spread my arms open wide to gather her into a long overdue embrace.

She takes three long strides toward me and if I was a smarter man, the look on her face would have warned me about what was going to happen next.

In one quick motion she steps up and drives the heel of her palm into my nose instantly breaking it and knocking me back a few steps.

She stares at me and I just stand there with blood trickling down my face onto my shirt. I have the feeling she is waiting for me to say something but fuck if I know what that something is at this point.

Then she bursts into tears and turns on her heels and walks away from us and out of the room.

Ten years go by and the view of her leaving is still a sight to behold.

"Oh I like her!" Twilla says and starts laughing her ass off, after a second or two Brain joins in.

I don't join them.

Twilla struts over and moving so fast that I have no hope of stopping her she resets my nose for me. It is all over in one brief savage blur of pain.

Not exactly the homecoming I was hoping for, but all things considered, not all that surprising, all things considered. The last time she saw me I used my borrowed Banshee powers to compel her to walk away and leave me to my death. She had walked away cursing me and it would appear that ten years had not mellowed her anger much.

That particular fence needed mending.

At least due to the deal me and the old man had made I was here with her to attempt that very thing. Without that I would still be slumbering on the Banshee Queens throne, dead to this world and losing even more time with those that I love. Losing even more time in the war against the vampires I had sworn my life to.

And then because the damn day hasn't been fucked up enough, my son walks into the room.

He is a slender, slightly built child with his mother's delicate features and skin the color of coffee with a dash of milk in it. Tall for his age and bald as a cue ball. His eyes are large and seem to shift between brown and hazel as he stands in the middle of the room. I notice with pride that he is wearing my old Firefly t-shirt, even though it is huge on him.

I glance over at Brain and he gives me a crooked smile that tells me he was the one that had passed on that particular legacy.

"Hello father." My son says calmly.

Swallowing hard I stand up and take a step or two toward him, I don't know how to do this. How to talk to the offspring I have never met? Where to begin? When Keela first told me she was pregnant, I had that moment of fucking panic that probably all new dads have, what the hell did I know about bringing a life into this world? I was not father material, hell I was just barely boyfriend material. But I had been prepared to step up and do my damn best when the fates determined otherfuckingwise. Now he stands before me, a living breathing reality. I wasn't there for him. Not my fault, not his fault, not anyone's fault really, just a cold as hell damn fact.

Never imagined I would first meet my first born child with a broken nose and blood drenched shirt, gifted to me by his mother.

Pretty sure Hallmark doesn't make a card for that.

Screw Hallmark.

"Hello yourself."

"I knew someone important to what we are trying to do was coming, I had no idea it was you. My powers work like that." He sounds vaguely apologetic to me.

I walk up to him and touch him gently on his shoulder without thinking and I have been trained better than that.

You never touch a clairvoyant without warning them first, so they can shield you out.

His eyes go wide and he flinches away from me in one spastic motion. I watch his eyes dart from me to Twilla and back again. A confused look flickers across his face and as I watch he closes his eyes and puts up his shield and pushes whatever he saw when I touched him away into whatever dark corner of his young mind he uses for such things.

"You and Brian have much to discuss. He knows all that I have told him and I must meditate on how you now fit into the plan we are forming." His voice is formal. He gives the both of us a small bow and hurries out of the room.

"I love children…but I can never finish a whole one." Twilla chimes in and then cackles with laughter as both Brain and I shoot her grim looks.

She sticks her forked tongue out at us and then curls up on a long table and goes to sleep.

CHAPTER SEVEN

"So he is calling the shots around here?" I ask Brain as I sit back down across from him.

"Not exactly, his visions give us valuable intel and he helps shape our plans. I have learned the hard way to listen to him." He tells me with old pain in his voice. His tone is flat with the subtext being he doesn't want to talk about what lesson was taught.

I give him a look and he bristles for a moment and then gives a weary shrug and tells me the story.

"He was no more than five and I was sending out a patrol to try and find some Order weapon caches. Little guy tugged on my sleeve and told me not to send them because growlers would tear them apart. I didn't listen and my people found what was left of the patrol the next day. They had been torn apart. We found them exactly where he said they would be. That was on me, those people died because I didn't listen to him." Old pain and regret adds tones to his voice I have never heard in it before. Being in command often sucks and things like this are the bloody price tag.

His people come back in and Jones puts a box in front of him. He nods his thanks at him and then unceremoniously shoves the box towards me.

"Keela gave me this a while after I told her what happened. For the record she broke my nose that day as well." There is a twinge of amusement in his tired voice.

I open the box and it is full of some of my old weapons.

Merry fucking Christmas.

I pull out my back up Hi-Point 9mm and greet it like the old friend that it is. Setting it aside I then pull out a Bond Arms Snake Slayer IV loaded up with 410 gauge buck shot and this brings another smile to my face. It is a custom job my old mentor gave to me and despite how that ended, I still love the weapon. Black hardwood grip with a blessed silver inlaid cross on each side. Next to come out is a high silver content blade blessed Bowie knife that fits my hand like it was made for it, which for the record it was by The Order's custom knife guy in the International District. Last but not least is the sawed off, double barreled, twelve gauge, that I so very long ago now, let Brain use to take out the vamp who had killed his wife. A handful of assorted cartridges and shells litters the bottom of the box.

"Thank you." I whisper.

"You have whatever ammo is in the box with the guns. We are dangerously low on weapons and ammo, but at least we still have a priest to bless our weapons. He is drunk the good majority of the time, but his blessings still seem to work." Brain tells me.

The Hi-Point goes to the small of my back and I slip the Snake Slayer into my jacket pocket. It is a relief to be armed once again.

The knife and its sheath go on my belt.

I consider the shotgun for a moment and then pick it up and toss it at Jones who catches easily and gives me a questioning look.

"Arm someone with it who needs a better gun."

He gives me a slow grateful nod and lays the gun on the table in front of him and sits there without saying a damn word.

Not a chatty bunch these guys.

"Talk to me." I tell Brain.

"Your son has roughed out a plan but to make it work we need supplies and weapons. I will give you the long story version privately later. Tonight we are going on a run to try and procure some of what we need, want to come with?" He gives me a wicked grin that reminds me of the old him, the man I trained. My best friend.

"I am sooooooooo coming with." Twilla says as she sits bolt upright on the table she was supposedly sleeping on, while eavesdropping on our every word. She does a backflip off of the table and lands in front of us.

Brain looks at me pointedly.

"She has certain skills and is damn hard to kill. I say bring her, she could be useful and not to be a dick, but how are you going to stop her?"

He considers it for a moment and then gives me a nod, I know him well enough to read in the subtext. She is my problem and my responsibility. If she somehow screws up, it is on my hands to fix it.

So be it.

I need to get my hands dirty, get back into the swing of things. Screw all this soul searching, reunions and emotionally charged meetings and reunions. Enough drama and trauma. Time to get back to what I do best.

Let us go forth now and fuck some shit up.

Praise the Lord and pass the ammunition.

CHAPTER EIGHT

"Ok people listen up, the kid has given us a lead on an old Order supply cache in Pioneer Square. Our mission is to raid that cache for every gun and bullet we can carry as well as a few specialty items we are hoping might be there. We are meeting an ally who will provide backup and support and hopefully help guide us in and out. We will be doing the cloaking spell that should help us not attract vamp attention but we will need to be on the lookout for growlers and Adepts." Brain begins to brief his little rag tag crew that now includes Twilla and myself.

Strange to be taking orders from my old trainee, but he has earned the right to lead these people and I haven't. Firefights are no place for egos.

"Joe, need to bring you up to speed on a few things that have changed since, well, since you left. Most of the older vamps don't bother hunting anymore they have enough blood slaves on hand, but some of the younger ones still like the hunt. The Resistance, aside from a few human scum bags known as sewer rats, are the only thing on the menu out on the streets. Also there are always a few castoffs who have displeased their makers who might be on the prowl. Last but not least there will be the damn growlers, go for head shots they can make way more damage than a normal dog. Move when we move, stop when we stop. Clear?" His voice is crisp and if there was any doubt that I will follow his orders, in it I can't detect it.

"Yes sir." I tell him calmly keeping my face neutral.

I don't know what he has told his people about me and Twilla but they are giving us a lot of sideways glances. She is all but vibrating in excitement, bouncing on the balls of her feet with a wild feral grin pasted on her face.

"Twilla, if you fuck up in any way, we will end you." Brain tells her in a casual matter of fact voice.

"Oh sweetie, I bet you say that to all the girls!" She tells him coyly batting her eyelashes at him.

Yeah, this is going to be fun.

"He pulls an old Ruger Blackhawk revolver out of a drawer in the desk he is standing next to and he offers it to her.

"No thanks big guy, I'm good." She demurs cheerfully putting her hands in her pockets.

He gives a strange look but then shrugs and hands the gun to a short black guy whose name I haven't caught yet.

There is a knock at the door and a woman helps in a very old man in a dirty suit with a dingy priest's collar. Even money if she is helping him because he is older than dirt or black out drunk. He proceeds to give a no doubt heartfelt but rather slurred blessing and then is carefully led back out again.

I watch Twilla's face during the blessing and notice her wincing in pain a couple of times. Even though she is a lesser imp she is still demonic enough not to enjoy the sound of sincere prayer and words of faith.

There are eight of us all together and without another word Brain leads us out the door and down yet another long tunnel.

Brain walks with a limp and I find myself wondering the story behind it. We need to sit down and catch up but right now there are bigger priorities, like living through this little mission for instance.

Yeah, let's start with that.

Twilla is all but vibrating with excitement and I hope that she will behave, for all of Brain's strong words about ending her, I doubt if this little rag tag army is up for it. She may be a lesser imp but she is still a creature embowed with demonic power, blessed rounds are going to hurt her but I doubt if they can utterly destroy her.

There is a slight twinge of pain in the eye that the old man swapped with me and I hope the twisted fuck is enjoying the show so far.

We move right along, this is old news for this crew and in short order we are emerging through a manhole cover out on the streets. I glance up at the night sky and there is an oily wrongness to the darkness that I now know is the spell sealing the city.

Shit goes wrong just about immediately.

Three growlers come padding around the corner and go ape shit when they catch our scent.

Motherfuckers are huge. About the size of Shetland ponies and with a hell of a lot more teeth. Things are nothing but dark fur wrapped around corded muscles. They come at us snarling and man are they fast.

Not as fast as Twilla though.

"Puppies!" She screams in delight and she moves past us in a blur and does a hand spring to land directly in front of the damn things.

They sniff at her confused for a moment by her non-human scent and I suppose by the fact that things don't usually run at them. They circle her slowly and then they spring at her.

I hold up a hand to stop all of the men with me from opening fire trying to save her because I know she doesn't need saving. They are all over her in a savage growling pile and she is barely visible through the creatures trying to tear her limb from limb.

And then she explodes.

The look on Brain's face is priceless.

The whole team just stands there in shock as various sized pieces of the growlers spatter against the street. As we all watch, the black goo that seems to be the essence of Twilla congeals back together.

"Ta da!" She announces as she reforms.

The rest of the guys are clearly impressed, I have now seen the show a couple of times.

Yeah, that's already getting old for me.

Hard to impress short attention spans.

We all move on, I see the looks his team shoots at Brain and I know he will be doing damage control later. That being said, we are all accustomed to weird shit happening and we move on. The team moves in a cautious steady pace out into the city. They move like the highly trained unit that they are, always alert and covering each other. Brain takes point and we all fan out behind him. All of us are moving double time now, the little show of Twilla's was loud and loud is the last thing we need right now, moving through the night time wasteland that used to be a city I called home.

My marks flicker at me and I pause for a moment to try and make sense of what they are telling me. A confusing trickle and massive wave of power are coming at me from what appears to be the same source. Never felt anything like it before.

A female vamp steps out of the shadows and glides slowly towards us with her pale slender hands up. She is of medium height with long dark hair and paper white skin, her clothing is standard issue Goth black and there is an air of fragility about her. I know her for what she is at once.

A starvling.

Such creatures are rare, generally they have been turned against their will and they are so repulsed by their new form that they take a vow not to feed on any living creature. The Order has recruited and used the pathetic things to get intelligence on the vampire community where they are mocked and sometimes slain out of hand. They don't live long or they give into the thirst and embrace their new existence.

This one is at least a hundred years old which is completely impossible.

I close one eye and look at her with the eye that the old man swapped out and I see a dark flickering around her of some kind. A seething sort of power nimbus that for all my training I cannot identify. She has an odd feeling of duality about her that is confusing the hell out of my senses. I want to ask Brain what the hell is up but this isn't the time for us to be playing twenty questions.

"Hello Andrea." Brain says softly motioning to all of us to lower our weapons and allow her to approach.

"Hello Brian, you travel in…interesting company this evening." She tells him in a muted toneless voice cocking her head first at Twilla and then at me.

"We have no time for introductions, are you prepared to lead us to the target?" He asks her crisply.

She gives him a long steady look but then shrugs eloquently and glides away from us back into the shadows.

It doesn't really seem like a very good idea, but we all follow her.

Straight into the waiting arms of a full coven of Dark Adepts.

I hate it when that happens.

CHAPTER NINE

Three of them instantly surround Twilla and cast a binding spell on her that slams her helpless to the ground. The rest fling curses at us that one by one drop us as paralyzed pain wracked wrecks unable to scream or writhe in the sudden agony we find ourselves in. Brain is the only one to get off a shot before he goes down but it is a total miss.

Andrea is the only one of us left standing and for a moment I think, she must have betrayed us somehow. That moment ends when the biggest Adept, a hulking balding middle aged man with a coven leader rune tattooed on his forehead steps up and backhands her hard across the face. As she lies on the ground he kicks her savagely a few times so hard that I can hear ribs snapping from where I am lying.

"Hello everyone, my name is Gary. I will be torturing, maiming and killing you all this fine evening." He says in a cheerfully mocking tone.

"Hello Gary." All his little coven brothers chirp back at him, all of them grinning in wicked anticipation of what is coming.

"We have noticed this pathetic little starvling bitch skulking about lately and being bored and having shit else to do. We decided to follow her and lo and behold it would appear that we have hit the jackpot! A band of stupid HRO cunts and believe it or not folks, an actual lesser demon!

There has to be a fun story behind all this and trust me before we are done you will be telling it to us."

Andrea manages to rise shakily to her feet, she is hurt and without feeding her vampire body will heal very slowly but never completely.

"You betray your own race and help these human scum? Tsk tsk little starvling. I hate your kind. Embrace the darkness within you, become more than you ever were in your sad little human life you cling to so miserably. I am taking the choice away from you, you will feed tonight. You can thank me later." He tells her as he picks up a scrap of wood from the ground.

He closes his eyes in concentration and I can feel him casting a dark shaping spell. The scrap of wood blurs and changes into a solid black baseball bat.

I tell my twitching fingers to raise my gun and blow his foul head off but they refuse. The pain curse disrupts all function and all I can do is lie there and twitch as he takes the bat and bashes Brett's brains in with it.

The bat is slick now with blood and bits of brain and he holds it out before her like someone at a cocktail party offering someone a tasty hor dourve.

"Lick it bitch." He tells her gleefully.

He knows that if she tastes the blood, the control she has over her thirst will likely break and the blood lust will come over her. There is no going back after that, she will be full vamp and all thoughts of revenge on those who turned her will fade away. All commitment to helping us against those who turned her will be broken and ended.

Even writhing in pain, I can feel that secondary odd energy churning around her and as I lie there wishing I could scream, I feel it intensify. There is a savageness to it that really wants to come out and play and I can feel the hand holding the leash on it start to loosen its grip. I can also feel the desperation of the hand holding that leash even if I can't understand it.

He backhands her again so hard that the slap sounds like a gunshot in the still of the night. She takes a step back and looks at him imploringly.

"I said lick it bitch!"

"Don't." She begs in a broken voice.

His face lights up with sick pleasure, nothing a bully loves more than the sound of his victims begging him for mercy. He is a Dark Adept and all mercy has long since fled the tattered remains of his soul. Turning to his boys he displays the bloody bat to them.

All of the coven is now laughing cruelly at her, except for the three binding Twilla, they are all business and concentrating on holding her in place. She may be a lesser demon but she is not to be trifled with, if they don't focus on the task at hand she could escape and they know what she is capable of. They are intrigued by what she is doing hanging out with the likes of us, but being the sick fucks that they are, they are going to have a little play time before they get down to the task of finding out why.

The energy whirling around Andrea reaches a crescendo and I can feel her losing control over it. My marks burn with a fire that rivals the curse binding me in place with pain.

"Damn you bitch you will feed! I command it! Lick the fucking bat you stupid cow of a starvling bitch!" Gary screams in frustration, he winds up to swing the blood soaked bat at her head.

There is a burst of power that ripples through the darkness surrounding us, I can feel it and I know that all of the Dark Adepts can feel it as well. They all give each other a confused look. Everything seems to stand absolutely still for a long second that is suddenly broken by a low throaty chuckle.

Andrea is standing there with her head downcast and she is standing there laughing. Her slight frame is actually shaking with laughter. The sound of it seems to echo off of the abandoned buildings surrounding us.

Except that it isn't Andrea anymore.

My marks tell me that someone, or something else has replaced her.

Someone or something far more fucking dangerous.

This should be fun.

He swings the bat at her head but it never connects. Her pale hand flashes out and stops it, casually she takes it away from him and tosses it aside. She looks up and her eyes now have a glowing red highlight to them that wasn't there before. All meekness has fled from her, raw strength and power has filled the vessel that had been Andrea moments ago.

In a blur of speed she is on him, fangs in his thick neck. She rides him down to the ground but he is drained before he hits it. Not content with that she twists his head around and around until it comes off in her hands.

She grabs the bat lying a few feet away from her and holding it in one hand and the head in the other she snarls at the coven surrounding her.

"Batter up!"

And then she tosses Gary's head up into the air and smacks it with the bat out into the darkness with a meaty thud. It goes sailing over the heads of the rest of the coven.

Which totally serves to break their concentration.

Twilla escapes with a surge of her will, she stand up and kills all three Dark Adepts guarding her in a blink of an eye, with the razor sharp claws that explode from her fingertips. Their guts splatter the ground and she howls in savage glee at their deaths.

Brain recovers before I do, he manages to raise his gun and blow out the brains of the Dark Adept closest to him.

Whatever Andrea has become tears through one of the bastards to get at the one behind him and then kills him just as dead. She pokes the bat right through the chest of the next idiot who rushes at her and then we are all free of the curses binding us and the next few minutes are an absolute slaughter.

I stick the Snake Slayer Derringer in the face of the fuck stain trying to run by me and take off his entire face.

Close range buckshot tends to do that.

The second shot goes into the groin of the asshole trying to crawl away from the mayhem after Twilla tore his left arm off. It ruined his whole damn day.

My borrowed eye burns and I know that the sick old fuck is enjoying the carnage, isn't this why he sent me back after all? Well me and the Dark Adepts have a long history of despising each other, so I don't begrudge him the damn show.

The Hi-point seems to leap into my hand and I start putting rounds into whatever targets present themselves. In seconds it is all over, they are dead and we, minus that poor bastard Brett are all still alive.

For the moment, we will call that a win.

Whatever Andrea has become stands in the middle of it all, her head is downcast again and my marks burn with the energies coming off of her.

Brain approaches her warily, his gun not exactly pointed at her but not exactly not pointed at her either. She stares him down as he approaches and without thinking my gun is now pointed right at her head. I look around me and so is everyone else's. Even Twilla is balanced on the balls of her feet ready to charge in if needed.

"Hello Dark Molly." Brain calls out calmly as he slowly approaches her.

"Fuck you Brian." She tells him just as calmly but with more than a hint of menace behind it.

"Fair enough. I need you to honor Andrea's promise to lead us to where we need to go tonight. We require your help." He tells her firmly. If he feels any fear he isn't showing it.

She glares at him, and I am proud that he doesn't even flinch before that awful stare. He stands his ground as I have taught him, hell, better than I have taught him.

"Very well, human scum. The other bitch who lives in my head says I have to help you. But know this, one day I will find a loophole in whatever pledge she gave you assholes and I will feast on your heart right in front of you." She hisses at him.

"And when that day comes Dark Molly, as I have told you before, I hope that you will choke on it. For now, take us where we fucking need to go. His voice has gone all alpha male and rings with command.

She trembles with rage before him and once again I am proud that he doesn't flinch before her, because she is a truly awful vision. Once again he stands his ground and returns her stare.

After a long terrible moment she gives him a slow nod and stalks off into the darkness, expecting us to follow her.

Once again, even though it feels like the poster child of all bad ideas, we all traipse behind in a ragged line.

"What the fuck just happened?" I hiss at my old friend as I catch up to him on our merry parade.

"It's a long story." He says wearily in a tone distinctly designed to discourage further questioning. With anyone else it likely would have worked but given our history it just plain old didn't.

"Then give me the God damned Readers Digest version." I put more force into my voice than I had intended to.

He turns to face me and for a moment I think that he is going to either shoot me or punch me in the face. I watch him win the struggle with his rage yet one more time and he draws a deep breath and answers me.

"Well ok Joe, here it is, do you want a fucking pen and paper so you can take some damn notes? Do you want me to speak slowly and use small fucking words? I mean I totally want you to be able to follow me on this. She was a novice White Adept who washed out of the training program due to some mental health issues. A sadistic fuck of an elder vamp turned her against her will, the trauma of that split her into two distinct personalities. One is Andrea, a starvling dedicated to helping the HRO to get revenge against the vamps who turned her. The other you just had the damn pleasure of meeting calls itself Dark Molly and is a force of fucking nature, a perfect storm of carnage. She keeps Andrea alive because she has no qualms about feeding. Andrea is a planner, Dark Molly is a buzz saw of violence. She is still on our side but just barely. Happy?" He barks at me.

"Well, no not really."

"Happy or not shut the fuck up and lets go get his done. Andrea would have led us cleanly past patrols and other assorted dangers, Dark Molly will still get us there but it will be a hell of a lot messier." With that he stalks away from me without a backwards glance.

Oh, that sounds encouraging.

Twilla comes skipping up to me with savage glee all over her face. She puts her hand on my arm and whispers into my ear.

"You sure know how to show a girl a good time."

I swing at her and I miss. Pissed off I try again and she just moves out of the way without really trying

And then she skips away ahead of me leaving a giggle echoing behind her.

Crap, everyone seems to be having more fun than I am.

One of the guys actually had the presence of mind to collect the weapons dropped by the slaughtered Dark Adepts. We already have more guns than we left with so we can already count this as a win, I suppose.

Except that poor bastard Brett, lying there with his brains, such as they were, splattered everywhere.

For him things sort of sucked.

I spare what is left of him a look and then I slap another magazine into my gun and follow my old trainee and a schizophrenic vamp into the darkness towards whatever the fuck we are looking for.

What the hell could go wrong with that plan?

Lacking a better idea, I move out to go find out the no doubt blood soaked answer to that particular question.

This whole being a team player thing has truly sucked so far.

As my Kindergarten report likely said, well hell in the interest of full disclosure it actually did say, I only know because my mother hung the damn thing on our refrigerator for all to see the final verdict of said teacher. I think that she and my father were equal parts proud and dismayed.

The report was clear and to the point.

"Joe does not work and play well with others."

True story.

CHAPTER TEN

We follow Dark Molly as best we can, she moves with more than human but less than vampire speed and even that compromise requires us to hustle to keep up. She doesn't spare us a backwards glance to see if we are behind her or not, because truth be told, she doesn't give a fuck.

She simply kills whatever she encounters. It is that simple. A newbie vamp who looks like a damn librarian goes for Brian and she slaughters it before he even knows it is after him. Some rag tag crew of what they called sewer rats challenges us at a street corner demanding a toll and in a blink of an eye they are all dead.

All five of them.

None of us fired a shot.

We are making too much noise and leaving too wide of a blood trail.

I lock eyes with Brain and he gives me a hopeless shrug. It is, after all, what it is. He would have preferred Andrea the tactician but he will make do with Dark Molly the undead buzz saw. Rule number one is that you work with what you have.

My trained eyes are picking up on the hidden runes pointing the way to wherever we are going. They are standard Order runes from my era and they say that a major ammo and weapon cache is just ahead of us. The runes also state that this is an area restricted to those with the very highest clearance. We follow Dark Molly through a doorway she casually kicks in and then we are following her down a series of stairs to way below street level.

Ever take the Seattle Underground Tour? Trust me this is below even that. No tourist has ever been where we are following the insane vamp now. A huge Pacific Islander vampire dude dressed in biker colors and sporting one of the worst mullets I have ever seen, challenges her at the second to last doorway. She just grins and guts him as casually as you and I might swat a damn bug. Then she tears his head off and tosses it aside and motions for us to pick up the pace. She stands there looking at us with her oddly glowing eyes daring us to not to follow her.

Jones shoots me a glance and all I can do is give him a nod and wave him ahead like it is a good idea to follow the crazy vamp. He looks skeptical but he moves out and what is left of our team follows him, no questions asked.

Back one day and I already hate my fucking job.

We head steadily downward through a system of dark stair cases, I look at Brain and see that he is reading the same runes that I am as we follow Dark Molly. I have no doubts that we are heading towards a weapon cache left by The Order. My doubts center instead around living long enough to get those weapons back to those who need them so desperately.

It is dark down here but my vampire taint and banshee heritage gives me excellent night vision. The rest of our little tribe lacks that advantage and one by one they whip out small penlights to light our path. Jones is the last one to resort to his but in the end he does the same. Twilla walks through the darkness like a virgin walking at high noon down the streets of the small town she has lived her whole life towards church on Sunday.

Well, maybe not quite like that.

More like a succubus doing the walk of shame from a frat boy's room in broad daylight.

Fuck it, screw metaphors she can fucking see in the damn dark, ok?

Dark Molly moves through the darkness like it owes her money or something. No hesitation, no looking back. She walks through the valley of shadows and she fears no evil because she is the absolute worst God damn thing in the whole fucking valley.

There was a time back in the day when that was my slogan but she totally owns it in her own right.

We walk through the dark in as much silence as we can muster for about an hour before we pause before a plain grey steel door set into the wall of the tunnel we are moving through.

The door is marked with runes that spell out that this is indeed a weapons cache. It is also marked with runes that say, access to it is limited to those with very high security clearances.

Which we don't happen to have.

"Any ideas?" Brain asks me in a low tone.

There is a number pad on the door and without a lot of hope, I try out the few access codes I can remember from the old days. After the first half dozen I give up doing things the easy way.

"Move your people down the tunnel, let's give Twilla a shot at it." I suggest with a shrug.

Turns out we are already testing Dark Molly's patience.

With a sound between a low hiss and a growl she shoves Brain out of the way and shoots out a pale hand and tears the whole fucking door off of its reinforced hinges and tosses it aside like a soda can.

She isn't old enough to be this damn strong, it just isn't possible. But I won't complain because the door is now open.

"Yay genius let's have the imp trigger a really loud explosion that will bring trouble down on us. Hurry you stupid fucks! We have a need for speed!"

As we all file into the room a motion detector triggers the lights and reveals the contents of the room.

Merry fucking Christmas.

There are cases of ammo, long boxes full of various forms of assault rifles, racks of handguns and a box or two of phosphorus grenades. There are also a few med kits and MRE meals by the shitload.

Brain ignores all this bounty and goes straight to the back of the room and places his hands on a wooden crate about the size and shape of a coffin. He stares at it with an unreadable expression for a moment before he begins barking orders.

"Everyone load up with as much as you can stuff in your backpacks. You and you make sure you get all the grenades. Take what you can carry and still be able to fight if we run into shit on the way back. Joe, you and I are carrying this and just this, as fucking carefully as we can."

"What the hell is it?" I ask as we pick the thing up, which by the way is heavier than it looks.

"Our last chance." He says under his breath looking me in the eye, his expression asking me not to slow things down with any more damn questions right now.

So be it.

Dark Molly watches us with a bored sneer on her face. She has not picked up anything to carry and nobody is dumb enough to test the seething energy boiling around her by asking her to. In a few minutes everyone is as laden down as they dare to be, even Twilla who is carrying at least twice as much as she looks like she can handle.

We haven't even made a dent in the supply.

Nobody is saying so, but the unspoken hangs in the room like a bad smell. We are leaving a lot of good stuff behind. Whatever Brain and I are carrying out of here had better be damn worth it. Our raid will be discovered and this treasure trove lost to us before we can return to it. This isn't sitting well with our merry band of adventurers but they are too disciplined to bitch about it here and now.

I put my end of the crate down for a moment and snag a few 9mm pistols and fill my pockets with ammo ignoring the look my old friend gives me. Then I pick my end up and nod to tell him I am ready.

"Double time people." Brain says crisply.

Dark Molly blurs out of the room and we all follow her back out and begin the long arduous process of following the imaginary trail of bread crumbs back up to street level.

Follow the fucking yellow brick road.

Vampires, growlers and Dark Adepts, oh my.

Brain and I are in the middle of the pack being protected by everyone else as we go. He whispered to me that if shit hits the fan to put down the crate as gently as possible and to protect it at all costs. We are moving so slow that I feel like a crawling turtle with a big target painted on my shell.

At least our protectors have decent weapons now, all the bullets will have been pre blessed before storage and some of the hollow points will have been filled with silver nitrate, essence of garlic and holy water bound in an absorbent polymer.

Twilla is carrying a lot of unloaded guns, the ammo seems to disagree with her.

My old friend is limping in obvious pain and he is sweating even though the night is cool, but he is holding up his end of the crate. His grim expression tells me that he will continue to do so until we are safely back or his guts are splattered all over the street.

After what seems like an eternity we are back up on street level. Dark Molly has apparently been busy while waiting for us for she stands in front of us splattered in new blood. She is licking her fingers casually as we catch up to her.

"Useless human fuck stains, you sound like a brass fucking band. Death wish or just plain old stupidity?" Her tone is bored and mocking with a sly undertone of barely contained menace.

In all my training and various misadventures, I have never encountered anything like her. When it comes down to it, all my training and so forth tells me that she is impossible.

Yet she stands before us licking blood off of her fingers and looking at us like we are dog shit she has just stepped in.

Then she looks right at me and for a moment I think that she is going to try and roll me with her eyes. Good luck with that, I have been immune to that little trick for a long time now.

Her eyes lock with mine and as I watch recognition replaces disdain on her alabaster face.

"Having fun yet Black Irish?" She asks me in a playful tone with an awful wicked grin.

Crap.

CHAPTER ELEVEN

Everything stops. Time slows to nothing as she and I stare at each other across the few yards that separate us. Neither Brain nor myself can go for a gun as we are carrying the crate. I flick a glance to my left and see Twilla almost oozing into position for an attack. She shoots me a glance telling me that all she needs is the barest nod from me.

Instead I give her a tiny shake of my head.

Whatever the vamp has up her sleeve I am too pissed off to care. Fuck whatever weird freak show the bitch belonged to. I keep one hand on the crate willing strength into that arm as I draw a gun in the other.

Been a long night, bring it bitch.

Instead we end our time with Dark Molly in much the way we began it.

She gives a low throaty chuckle and then collapses all at once like a marionette after a samurai sword slices in Hollywood slow motion through the strings holding it up.

The seething storm of arcane energy flickers away to nothingness to be replaced by the slow trickle of power flowing weakly from her. She is once again the starvling that we met, she is once again Andrea. Somehow she has freed herself from the otherling living in her head.

I put my gun away and grab the crate with both hands again. As I do so I catch Brain in a single glaring unguarded moment and for that brief instant a look of unabashed tenderness washes over his face so quickly I might be able to make myself believe that I imagined it.

Except that the same look is mirrored on Andrea's face for that same instant. She looks down in equal parts grief and horror at the blood staining her hands and a shiver of revulsion shakes her slight frame. Bowing her head she takes a moment to pull herself together and when she looks up, her face is the same alabaster mask that she first greeted us with.

"Follow me." She says blandly and then she turns to glide away from us and once again we are following her pale form through the darkness that lies between us and relative safety.

All this is very interesting and will definitely turn up as bullet points in the long conversation that my former trainee and myself will be having very damn soon. Another bullet point will be how his little schitzo vampire lady friend knew me by name. We will discuss all this and more but for now we will focus on the task at hand.

Getting home alive.

Yeah, let's start with that.

Forgot one more damn bullet point, what the hell is in this crate I am carrying so carefully? Why does my old friend seem to think that it's so fucking important and worth such risk to bring back?

A decade has passed and one damn thing has remained constant and completely unchangeable.

I have no idea fucking idea what the hell is going on.

On that cheerful mental note we all move this show down the road.

We move slowly but steadily, Andrea flickers in amongst us at intervals to steer us away from assorted dangers. A full coven of Dark Adepts and a handful of vampires and other assorted victim have been slaughtered. This is the equivalent of kicking a hornets nest and reprisals will be raining down on us soon enough. Hopefully we can make it back home before the storm gathers and the lightening starts to strike.

Or not.

A massively built black vamp of just under two hundred years steps out of a narrow alley and blocks our path. He is wearing a form fitting tuxedo complete with top hat.

Jones reacts first and shoots the vampire in the head seven times as fast as he can pull the trigger with one of the new guns we just scored.

I decide, I like Jones.

The vamp goes down but not for long enough. He swipes a hand suddenly armed with razor sharp claws at Jones but misses because Jones is already diving backwards and slamming another clip home.

Another smaller vamp darts out of another alley but Andrea is suddenly between us and him baring fangs and hissing at him so violently that I start to think Dark Molly is back.

But no. My marks tell me that this is still the starvling not the undead buzz saw alter ego.

Things are going south fast, I hear several guns firing now and I shoot a look at Brain that he needs to be making a call right the hell now or I will use my best judgment.

Nobody wants that.

He shakes his head at me grimly. I take him at his word and just that fast we aren't in this fight.

Which sucks.

The short black dude empties his Ruger Blackhawk into the chest of the older better dressed vamp and then he dances away to reload, this isn't anyone's first day at the rodeo.

Twilla appears behind the younger vamp and with a gleeful giggle she reaches out and tears the damned things unbeating heart out and then drops it to the dirty ground and starts to stomp on it. She pauses for a moment to kick what is left of the vampire back into the shadows of the alley and then goes right back to stomping.

Got to admire her work ethic anyway.

Give vamps a couple of centuries of undead life and they start getting damn hard to kill, sunlight is a surefire but not of much help in our current situation. The vamp is struggling back to its feet after having at least twenty blessed bullets blasted into it. Maybe the blessings are past their expiration date or something cause they aren't doing the damn trick.

"Switch too your old weapons!" I bark out as the vamp starts to move towards Jones.

A shaggy headed young guy with an annoyingly wispy goatee lets loose with the sawed off shotgun I had tossed at Jones and the vamp goes back down. The kid takes a couple steps closer and lets the vamp have it again pretty much point blank into its face.

Problem solved.

We are on the move again and Andrea haunts us like a ghost, not really with us, just appearing from time to time to move us around various dangers. In the not far away enough distance, we can hear the howls of growlers as we clamber down the passage we had climbed up to get to street level.

Home again home again jiggity jig.

The priest is there as we return and repeats his slurred blessings over us as we all file back in. He is being held up by a different woman this time and she stares at him with a sad expression that contains a sense of loss I had no context for. We all stow the pickings of the raid away, Brain and I locking the crate we had carried into a small store room.

Exhaustion starts to hit me as the adrenaline rush of the time starts to fade in me. It has been, well let's just say a hell of a day.

"Joe, don't know what the fuck to say brother. Nice to have you back from the grave. We will talk privately in the morning, we both have things we need to say and ask." Brain says as he gives my shoulder a squeeze as he limps past. I watch him as he goes and my muddled brain gives up trying to wrap itself around all that has happened. Time to go fall down for a while. Way past time actually.

The day begins to catch up with me more and more, the last time I felt this exhausted it didn't end well.

Jones steps up and grabs my arm to point me in the direction of a bed. He looks even more rung out than I feel and after telling me where to go he staggers off to whatever bed he calls his own. Twilla curls up on the same table top she pretended to fall asleep on earlier.

"Five doors down, it is marked bunk house six. The guy using if before, well he don't need it no more. Thanks for joining the party whoever the fuck you are." He calls back at me. His voice is hoarse with his own weariness and he is shaking his head and muttering under his breath as he walks away from me.

Sleep pulls at me and I shuffle down the hallway in the direction Jones pointed me in without even throwing an insult or two at him.

Really not like me.

I look back at Twilla and she is lying there with her eyes closed and a know it all smirk on her face. If I wasn't so damned tired I would go back and either find out what she is smirking about or failing that, knock the damn smirk right off of her impish face.

Yeah, not happening tonight.

Instead I keep on shambling down what has to be the longest hallway in the collected history of hallways towards the bunkroom Jones pointed me towards and I turn the knob and step into the room.

To find out that somebody is already there.

CHAPTER TWELVE

The room is pretty bare bones, a beat up mattress on top of a beat up box spring on the floor. A single unshaded bulb illuminates the room and she is standing directly under it as I step into the room.

She stares at me with an unreadable expression on her face, the harsh light of the bare bulb reveals lines in her face that weren't there when I compelled her to walk away from me all those years ago. The lines don't detract from her beauty, they in some way seem to frame it. The lines speak of strength, of challenges met and overcome. They are worn proudly as should anything that is earned at costs that nobody would ever guess at.

We stand there staring at each other, the room is small and we could touch one another if we made the slightest effort. I ache to, I truly do but my broken nose aches too as a reminder that touching her is not a right I am entitled to right now.

The moment stretches out past its breaking point finally.

"I am sorry I broke your nose." She tells me in a small voice with her eyes now cast downward.

"Not the first time it has been broken." I remind her gently.

She slowly takes the few steps separating us and then reaches out a hand to trace the length of my nose.

"Is it really you?" She asks me staring into my eyes. I can hear more things in her voice than I have names for. Hope, regret, pain, sorrow, anger, guilt to name a few.

I answer her the only way that seems possible just now, the only form of communication that makes any sense that offers any hope of expressing what I need to tell her.

I kiss her.

There is a moment of resistance, I feel her body tense and for a horrible instant I think she is going to push me away.

Then she kisses me back.

Enthusiastically.

Sleep will just have to wait for a little while longer.

A lot longer actually. Our lovemaking was as spectacular as always and afterwards we held each other and tears were shed.

Not ashamed to say that some of those tears were mine.

Our connection has always been strong, every time we have been together we have treated it like it may be the last time because considering the lives we led it very well could have been. Touching her had been its own special sort of homecoming and I still can't wrap my head around the fact that it has been ten years since I have.

She sleeps curled up into me but despite my exhaustion sleep still eludes me. My brain whirls with all that has happened since I dropped back into this world. There is too much that I don't know and what you don't know is usually what ends up biting you in the ass. Ten years out of the loop leaves a lot of things these guys take for granted that I don't know fuck all about.

One of the things that baffles me is Andrea/Dark Molly. In all my years as a Gun I have never encountered anything remotely like her. She is a complete impossibility yet she exists. The whole split personality thing aside, my marks tell me that she has been a vampire for a hundred years but she is far too powerful to be that young. The way she tore the door to the weapons cache off its damn hinges suggests that she is three times that old but my marks have never been wrong.

Another fun question, how the fuck did she recognize me? I know I have never run across her during my time with The Order. I have been thought of as dead for ten years now in both the human and the vampire world. I have to be careful, ten years is a blink for the older vamps and if one of them sees me they will know me. I got up a little while ago and used the tiny bathroom attached to the room and took a good long look in the mirror. I look exactly the same as I did ten years ago, for me time has more or less stood still.

Brain and I will talk tomorrow and I will get some answers, the process may seem a little one sided to him because the old man put some serious mojo on me keeping me from giving up any details of how I came back to this world. I tested it on Keela and I literally couldn't make myself tell her the truth. Instead I spun her the same bullshit story about wandering lost in the shadows and encountering Twilla, who for no good reason decided to help me find my way out and hang out with me for a while.

She had given me a look that told me she knew I was lying but somehow understood that I was telling her all that I could. After a long moment she had changed the subject and started telling me about our son.

Tumaini.

He had been different from the day he had been born. By the time he was one he was speaking in complete sentences and by two he was demonstrating his clairvoyant talents. Brain had, as promised, watched over them and when things started to go to shit he moved them to a series of safe houses. Nobody saw the whole Dark Adepts sealing the city bit coming or otherwise he would have gotten them completely out of the city. Well, as it turns out, almost no one. The boy had tried to warn everyone that he had dreamed about the dark stain filling the sky and trapping everyone but no one had listened.

Now the kid was the lynch pin of the whole resistance, his visions giving the intel needed to try to not only survive but to try and somehow retake the city and end the occupation. Brett had not been alone in labeling the kid a freak, people fear what they do not understand but if such things bothered him, my son apparently had never shown any sign of it.

For the last year or so Keela told me he had been suffering from nightmares from which he would wake up screaming the same thing every time.

"What began in blood will end in blood."

He claimed not to remember the dreams or know what the phrase meant but Keela had likely given him the same look she had given me, the one that said I know you are lying but I know you have your reasons.

My eyes finally close from their own weight and sleep finally claims me, pulling me under in a slow dark tide.

I am so tired that the usual nightmares that tend to await me are replaced by sheer oblivion. The last thing I feel before going under is a twinge of icy pain in the eye the old man swapped out.

Good night you miserable fuck, hope you are getting your damn jollies and enjoying the show so far.

When I wake up Keela is gone, just the scent of her lingering on the sheets to tell me that the night before hadn't just been a dream. I get up and get dressed which includes holstering a couple of guns.

Then I go looking for Brain.

I walk back down the hallway into the mess hall area and before I walk half a dozen steps Twilla is skipping next to me and chirping at me.

"Good morning big guy! How are we this bright and sparkly morning?"

God help me, I managed to draw a demonic imp that is also a fucking morning person.

Fuck me gently with a chainsaw.

I grunt at her and move past her praying that there will be coffee.

"Oh, somebody is just a little grumpy pants this morning! Didn't sleep so well did we? Did maybe something come up during the night?" She purrs at me in a sinfully innocent tone.

Please God, let there be coffee.

Brain comes to my rescue walking up and handing me a big mug of hot black coffee and pointing me towards the store room that we locked the crate in last night. Twilla starts to follow and without speaking he sticks a large revolver in her face and shakes his head slowly. He makes a slight shooing motion with the hand not holding the gun and for a change she takes the hint and backs away slowly.

"Wow, two grumpy pants this morning! Cheer up fellows, today is the first day of the rest of your life!" She gives us a lurid wink and prances away to sit down next to Jones who gives her a sour look as he drinks his own coffee.

We walk into the room together and he motions me towards one of the several chairs arranged around the big ass conference table we had set the crate on last night.

Instead of sitting, I whisper a simple seeking spell under my breath and release it at the crate. Immediately it pings back at me letting me know that whatever is in the crate has a slight nimbus of white magic around it.

Interesting.

"Talk to me, old friend." I tell him softly.

"Things went bad really quickly Joe, especially after the Dark Adepts pulled off their little trick. The Order collapsed within days, every elder vamp out there starting killing Guns on sight until there just weren't enough of us to do anything about it. The tattered remains of The Order went underground and formed the HRO and we are even more fucking tattered now." Brain's voice is strained and bitter sounding.

"What's in the box Brian?" I ask him calling him by his real name for one of the first times since we met all those years ago.

"Morton oversaw the project along with a handful of techs and some of the few remaining White Adepts. It is a combination of magic and technology Joe that will likely never be achieved again. We lost track of it until now, until your son's visions steered us towards it. Now that we have it we can move ahead with our plan." Brain tells me as he hands me a small pry bar and motions towards the box.

"What the fuck is in the box?" I ask him through clenched teeth.

"It is a vampire nuke. When detonated it will emit a magically enhanced burst of UV radiation for exactly thirty seven seconds. Any vamp no matter how ancient within the blast radius will be a crispy critter, once the vamps die, so will their human servants." Brain says once again gesturing towards the crate again.

Well now, things are looking up.

I use the pry bar and pop the crate open, packed in foam peanuts inside is a grey metal tube about four feet long attached to a crystal globe, about the size of a basketball. A timer with three buttons underneath is set into the tube about halfway down.

"The plan?" I ask as I lift the thing carefully out of the crate, the damn thing is far heavier than it looks. I put it down oh so very damn carefully on the table.

"The blast area is limited in scope so without the right timing the thing is useless to us. Your boy tells me it has to happen three nights from now or it won't happen at all. Just so happens that his timeframe coincides with the annual shit fest the vampires throw on the anniversary of the fall of Seattle at Safeco field."

I give him a skeptical look.

"No shit Joe, they throw a party complete with fucking Roman gladiator games. Humans against growlers, humans against newbie vamps, humans against humans. All the elders attend with their human servants and assorted guests. The bare bones of the plan is to infiltrate the stadium, plant the nuke and then at the right time detonate it. The blast will make crispy critters of every vamp in its range, we will play clean up with the new guns and grenades. We will kill as many of the fucks as we possibly can and hopefully even the odds for us. The other half of the plan is less concrete, after we fuck them up as much as possible, the kid says he can somehow disrupt the Dark Adepts barrier spell."

"How do we crash the party? After Dark Molly called me out it occurred to me that my face is pretty much well known to the local vamp hierarchy." I ask him hoping he has some ideas.

The look on his face tells me that what I just told him hadn't even been on his radar.

"I can help with that." Twilla tells us both cheerfully as she steps out of a shadow in the back of the room.

Brain pulls his gun and fires at her but the shot goes wild, he doesn't miss much so I figure she did some sort of mojo.

"You ever hear of knocking?" I ask her tensely.

"Sorry boys, my bad." She giggles and does a backflip back into the same shadows she just stepped out of vanishing completely.

Sure enough like ten seconds later there is a knock at the door.

Brain gives me a look that would scare me if I wasn't so damn tough and all and in return I give him a helpless shrug.

With an exaggerated sigh he stomps to the door and opens it and she skips in merrily past him.

"You said something about helping." I remind her through clenched teeth that grind down even harder when she winks at me and blows me a kiss.

She walks up to me and puts one hand on either side of my face, she has to reach up on tippy toes to do it.

"Sorry big guy, this is going to hurt like hell." The sawed off little bitch doesn't sound remotely sorry.

She isn't wrong.

It does hurt like hell.

CHAPTER THIRTEEN

A moment of bone searing agony consumes my face and I fall to my knees from the force of it. Imagine every bone in your face being slowly crushed and then the jagged pulp that once was what you looked at in the mirror every day, shifted and reformed.

Then imagine someone kicking you hard in the balls on top of the above mentioned torment.

"Go look big guy." She tells me as she pulls me to my feet and shoves me in the general direction of the mirror and sink in the corner of the room.

I am almost afraid to look.

The difference is subtle but the effect is profound. My nose is smaller and unbroken, my lips thinner and my chin more rounded. My skin is just a shade or two paler than usual and a thin stubble of hair covers my formerly bald head. All this might not sound like much but in the end the effect completely makes me all but unrecognizable.

Twilla skips up to me and whispers a guttural word in my ear three times and I feel it lodge in my brain.

"Simple, say that word under your breath three times and you can shift between this face and your own, and yeah it will hurt that bad every single time. Pain is the price of magic after all."

And of course I have to test the theory.

Of course she is right and I almost puke from the pain this time but my old face now stares back at me from the mirror.

"You are welcome." She tells me primly with a mocking glance.

"Thank you Twilla." I tell her formally tossing in a slight bow. Funny thing is that I mean it, pain aside I am all out of Groucho Marks glasses or for that matter any sort of disguise so, pain aside I am grateful for her help.

An odd expression dances briefly across her face and she turns away from me and steps back into the shadows without another word and disappear into it.

Brain is giving me a look that telegraphs that he is about to ask me all sorts of awkward unanswerable questions about what is up between Twilla and me and just how exactly did I manage to find my way out of the shadows.

The best fucking defense is always a good offense.

I beat him to the punch.

"What the hell is up between you and the starvling?" I demand.

He actually blinks at me in total confusion at the sudden change of topics. A slow blush travels across his lined face that makes him look older and sad.

"Nothing, nothing at all Joe, but hey thanks for asking." He spits the words at me, bitterness coloring his tone.

A tense moment hangs in the air between us, fraught with tensions old and new. My old mentor, the one who both trained and betrayed me used to sum it up with one of his countless sayings.

"Go ahead asshole, make a choice. Fight, fuck or go for your gun."

In the end he picks none of these options. Instead we are interrupted by yet another knock at the door.

Brain curses under his breath and turns his back solidly on me and stomps over to the door and pulls it open ready to tear Twilla a new one.

My son stands in the doorway looking at us solemnly.

"The time has come." He tells us.

And then he faints dead away falling into a crumpled heap on the cold hard floor.

Brain whips out a restraining hand to stop me from touching the little guy again and likely making whatever is going on worse. I give him a nod to let him know that I appreciate it but we still have unfinished business.

He returns the nod and settles himself on the floor near to but not touching my son and gestures for me to do the same. I do so and after a few seconds the boy stirs weakly and then hauls himself into a sitting position. His eyes have odd highlights in them and his slight form seems to thrum with hidden energies. I can feel power coming off of him in sharp edged waves.

Twilla appears in the doorway with a no doubt clever remark ready for delivery. Without sparing her a glance the boy gestures slightly with his right hand and she is picked up and flung away from the door to smack into a wall on the far side of the next room. At the exact same instant the door to this room slams closed.

Apparently he is a powerful telekinetic as well as a clairvoyant.

"On the day of the celebration the agents we have planted in the blood camps are going to stage full on riots. These riots will force the Dark Adepts to abandon the security detail guarding the stadium to go help quell the riots giving us the chance to infiltrate and plant the bomb. They are, so very brave. The reprisals will cost hundreds of human lives. This will be the last stab of our resistance, our last stand and last chance. All lies in the balance."

Tears are running down his face and I know that his visions are showing him the scores of humans who will die in the camps to buy us this chance. My heart aches for him, this is a bitch of a burden for a child to carry.

He struggles to his feet and walks over to look at the vampire nuke setting on the table. His expression is unreadable as he stares down at it and his hands are firmly in his pockets, he doesn't seem to want to touch it.

"Do you know how to operate it?" He asks Brain in a soft voice.

"Pretty straight forward, set timer and hit the arming button. When the timer goes off a levitation spell will float it up to the proper height and it will emit its enhanced UV burst until its power source is exhausted. We need to get it into the stadium and plant it in a more or less central location to maximize the effectiveness of the burst."

"Select a team, mother and I will be coming along. This is not open for debate, it is necessary for reasons I can't explain." The boy tells us in a stronger voice looking us both in the eyes.

Going to feel like old times, Keela, Brain and I used to go out on patrol during the vampire/banshee war and we made a hell of a team. Not thrilled about the kid going but then again he isn't exactly a helpless child. If he says it is necessary, I tend to take him at his word and if this is indeed our last chance against the vamps, we need every edge we can get.

I half expect Brain to argue the point but after a moment he just shrugs and gives the kid a nod.

Twilla steps out of the shadows and she isn't happy.

"Excuse me but did the little runt just slam me into a wall? Rude!" She hisses as she starts to walk up to him. Her claws are out and I am ready to intervene if she tries to use them.

I don't get the chance to.

He gestures wearily and slams her into the wall again and this time holds her there about halfway up. She struggles and curses but she can't free herself.

"Listen to me carefully, creature. In my visions you accompany us so even though I don't trust you, it would appear that you will be coming on the mission. Do anything that hints at betrayal and I will tear you apart molecule by molecule to the point where you will never reassemble yourself."

His voice is as cold and unforgiving as steel and as he speaks he walks slowly towards her. When he is a few feet away he clenches his fist and she starts screaming.

"And I will keep you alive and writhing in agony every single moment of the process."

With that nasty promise he unclenches his fist and she drops like a rock to the floor. He doesn't spare her a glance as he turns and walks out of the room, hell he doesn't spare me a glance either for that matter.

He is just a little bit scary.

"Make sure the priest blesses all the new weapons." He tells Brain over his shoulder as he walks out.

Twilla gets to her feet slowly and stares daggers at the doorway he just walked through.

"The kid is a complete asshole." She mutters.

"Like father like son." Brain chirps giving me the goofy as shit eating grin he used to flash me in the old days. It both cheers and depresses me, it is great to see flashes of my old friend but I know he had the shit kicked out of him over and over again while I have slept. I know the kind of burden he has been carrying all these long years. He goes so far as to stick his tongue out at me.

For some reason that strikes both of us as hilarious and we start laughing, Twilla is less amused and after shooting us both dark looks she stomps off back into the shadows and disappears.

Neat trick but not one I am tempted to try my hand at again.

Brain and I then sit down and start working out a plan for crashing the vampires little party and then retaking the city we both swore vows to protect. According to the kid the fate of everyone trapped here is in our hands.

Great, no pressure then.

CHAPTER FOURTEEN

Keela comes to my room for the next two nights, I don't see much of her during the day as Brain and I have been cobbling a plan together. He has always been a brilliant planner and strategists and whatever he has been through while I have been gone has not changed that.

I have been trying to connect with my son but he seems to be avoiding me, really easy for a clairvoyant to do since they know you are coming into a room before you get there. For all that, I catch him a few times watching me from across rooms. I tell myself to take it slow and not crowd him, Keela tells me the same thing. She also tells me to remember that he isn't a typical child, hell from what she tells me he named himself before birth. Story has it he whispered his name into her dreams every night for a week or so before he was born.

She tells me that she has no idea what it means. He always tells her that he will tell her at 'the proper time'.

Yesterday he told her that he would tell both of us what it meant very soon now. Has he been waiting for me to tell her? Beats the shit out of me Sherlock.

Brain comes into our conference room carrying what he went out to get, he went out alone against common sense and every single person's advice to meet Andrea who was to give him what we needed. Jones in particular seemed to think it was a stupid idea and pressed the issue to the point that Brain had to order him to back off.

Yeah, I like Jones.

He has a stack of dayslave overalls.

Dayslaves, I have been told, are humans culled from the pack to serve the vampires as more than just a food source. The old plantation slavery system before the civil war had field slaves and house slaves. Dayslaves are pretty much just house slaves. They do the work Dark Adepts and human servants consider beneath them and they all wear bright orange overalls with their master's glyph on the back. This is for discouraging other vampires from attacking them because they are supposed to be off limits.

It is considered bad form in vampire culture to interfere with another vampires servants.

Not that it doesn't happen.

So posing as a work crew of dayslaves, we will infiltrate the stadium and plant the nuke. We will also stash guns and grenades and wait for the vampires to be in their seats, for the nights fucked up entertainment, to detonate the bomb. After it goes off, we will kill as many surviving vampires, human servants and Dark Adepts as we can and then retreat.

Easy peasy lemon squeezy.

That is part one of the plan, hit the vamps hard and fast doing as much damage as possible. Part two isn't nearly as concrete. The kid says that this is his department and that he has a way to undo what the Dark Adepts did to seal the city. When we press him for details he gets all stoney faced and starts talking about things like 'probability matrixes' and 'conflicting paradoxes' until we go away. All he will really say is that the more vamps, human servants and Dark Adepts we kill the more chance he has of succeeding in his part. All that death, will somehow give him what he needs to bring the barrier down.

Once it is down, I know that The Order will flood the city with Guns before the government can even get soldiers in and do as much clean up as possible. Even after all this time I know that they are monitoring the barrier and will be in position to move in as soon as the barrier fails. Even with their spin doctors there will be no way to conceal that vampires had held the city captive. Too many witnesses to that awful fact. The vampire world will no longer be hidden in the shadows, humankind as a whole will be made aware of their existence.

What will come of that, there is no way for us to know and truth be told, not something we are sparing much thought to just now.

One fucking disaster at a time.

The stadium will be a blood bath, the nuke will help even the odds for us but with that many elder vamps there, a few will survive long enough to kill some of us. Hell, maybe even most of us. No point sparing that much thought either, it is what it is. We will fight them until we die or they all do. My son will then do whatever it is that he has planned. We owe it to the poor bastards who will be dying in the blood camps to give us this shot to do every damn thing we can to make sure that their sacrifice is not in vain.

I am calm. I long ago accepted the fact that I would not die of old age peacefully in my sleep. In the life I have lived the possibility of violent death has stalked me from the first day and I have already cheated death once.

The eye the old man swapped with me gives me a stab of pain, I think he does it on purpose from time to time to remind me that he is watching. I hope the miserable old bastard has been enjoying the show, the grand finale is coming right up and I am sure that he will enjoy the carnage to come.

"Give me a hug Joe." Twilla says as she bounces up to me.

"Why the hell would I do that?" I ask her, honestly curious.

"Because there is just no way I can walk in there with you crazy kids, any stray Dark Adept and some of the older vamps will know me for what I am at a glance. I need to fade back into the tattoo on your, oh so very muscular arm where I can pass unnoticed." She gives me a wistful smile and stands before me trying hard to look innocent and harmless.

Failing miserably of course.

What the fuck, in for a penny in for a pound and all that crap.

So I give the little shit a hug.

"Remember what I told you the price of magic was." She tells me with a wicked grin as she steps into my arms.

Fuck me gently with a chainsaw, but it hurts. She blurs out of focus and shifts into her black goo form and more or less pours herself onto the spot on my arm where the old man first marked me. It feels like someone pouring concentrated acid on my skin. If I wasn't so damn tough I would be screaming right now.

Oh the hell with it, I did scream.

More than a little.

Then it is over and she is just a mark on my arm.

Brain and Jones come running up to see what all the noise is about and I just point at my arm and wave them away.

They exchange a glance but they don't press the issue. I walk away from them heading back to my room and when I come around the corner my son is standing there waiting for me.

"Hello father." He greets me calmly.

"Hello yourself." Yeah, I am pretty known for my clever bantering skills.

We stand there for a long moment just looking at each other. He looks like hell actually, the strain of all this is telling on him. I am proud of him, he carries a burden that would overcome a lot of strong full grown men and he carries it with grace.

"This is for you. It has been blessed by our priest and dipped in holy water. It will…afford you some privacy if you follow my meaning." He tells me solemnly as he hands me a black eye patch.

I take it from him carefully so I don't accidently touch his bare skin. Shrewd little guy seems to have figured things out from when I touched him last time. His eyes drift to the new tattoo on my arm and he nods slightly.

I put on the eye patch covering up the old man's eye and cheating him of his show for the time being. That should serve to piss him off. Fuck him if he can't take a joke.

"Arrrh Matey! Yo ho ho and a bottle of rum. Shiver me timbers." I give him my truly awful pirate imitation.

For a split second a grin flashes across his face and for that one instant he looks like the child he never got the chance to be. It makes my heart ache to know what he has been cheated out of by the fucking vampires and their Dark Adept lap dogs. I will take the patch off and give the old man his damn show back as I kill as many of them as I can, but it is nice to have a respite from the connection between us.

I can lie down with my girl one more time at least and the old bastard has no right to be a voyeur to that.

"Thank you." I tell him simply.

Instead of answering he stares back at me for a long moment, it seems like he wants to tell me something but doesn't quite know how. I return his gaze as calmly and patiently as I can. If there is something he wants to say I am here to listen.

But after a few seconds he turns away and walks slowly back the way he came without saying a word. I watch him go not knowing what to say or do.

We are after all strangers to each other.

I walk to my room and open the door and see Keela waiting for me on the small bed.

"Shiver me timbers wench." I tell her with a savage grin.

She giggles at me and it is the sweetest sound that I have ever heard.

CHAPTER FIFTEEN

It is show time. All of us are in our dayslave overalls and we are shuffling towards a service entrance of the stadium with our eyes servilely downcast. We are trying hard to mimic the cringing body language of the steady flow of real dayslaves we are walking with. Wolves slinking alongside sheep. Including Keela and our son, there are nine of us.

Nine desperate wolves.

I said the words Twilla whispered in my ear and with a bone wrenching spasm of pain I am wearing another face. One that will hopefully pass me unnoticed past the eyes of the human servants and Dark Adepts guarding the entrance we will soon be trying to gain access to. I can see them from here, cruelty spelled out in the harsh lines of their faces. Eager hands clutching evil looking whips, eyes darting amongst the sheep hoping for a target.

Too long without a real target and their eagerness spills out and they slash their whips randomly into the crowd to find whatever flesh they happen to slash across. Every few minutes like bloody clockwork a scream rings out.

My hands ache from the need of pulling my guns and blowing big fucking holes in these assholes. I grind my teeth and force myself to idly listen to the screams as I plod closer to the entrance.

Brain had warned me what to expect. Warned me that if the whip happened to strike me, I was to endure it and keep on walking. He had pointedly reminded me that brave men and women in the blood camps were being slaughtered to buy us this chance.

Warned me not to let my pride and rage force me to blow my cover.

I promised him I wouldn't, it will be a harder promise to keep if the whip lash strikes Keela or my son.

But keep it, I will.

So we move with the flow and the fear of the lash coming down, at least it will add credibility to our submissive cringing shuffle.

My marks are still now, but come night I know that they will be on fire with the presence of so many vamps, so many elder and ancient vamps. I will have to call upon all of my training to push that aside and stay focused on the mission we came here to attempt. I am a fully trained Gun and no matter how badly they burn, I will do what we came here to do.

The boy is behind me and to my left. Sadly he is not the only child in the shuffling line we are following. Scattered throughout the throng are far too many small slight forms. I hear him mutter, mostly to himself in a tiny sad voice.

"It has begun."

Sure enough, there is a sudden flurry of activity at the entrances and we see the Dark Adepts peel away to go charging off into the shadows. In a matter of seconds they are all gone leaving only the human servants standing guard. They have a German concentration camp sort of efficiency and they manage to spread themselves around to fill the gaps and the line starts forward again with barely a hiccup.

The whipping is abruptly halted by the sudden exit of Dark Adepts. The human servants are all business as they pass along us.

Doesn't make them any less dangerous.

We pass under their sharp gaze and after what seems like a grueling slow motion eternity, we move past them.

The stench of this many unwashed humans is appalling and works in our favor as the human servants wave us by them holding scented clothes to their faces. The look of disgust they give us as we pass doesn't hold a tenth of the disgust I feel towards them.

They are all going to die.

Beneath our overalls we are carrying as many weapons as we could possibly get strapped to ourselves. We each have a couple grenades we are saving for a special occasion.

Say a vampire BBQ.

We tense up as we approach the second level of security. Brain and I are slowly pushing a janitor cart containing the vampire nuke and assorted other bits of mayhem. The rest are arranged around us in a rough circle. The human servant ahead of us, checking out each slave entering, is an older Asian woman and she is taking the job seriously as hell.

"Halt! Stand for inspection!" She barks at us and with a wave of her hand two armed human servants take up position around us. We stop in our tracks and drop to our knees as Andrea had informed Brain was the protocol.

She stalks around us, I don't know what but something about us has blipped her radar. I don't think she even knows what it is, maybe we aren't humble or filthy enough. Doesn't matter, if we can't make it past her then our cause is lost and we are finished before we even start.

My son stands slowly up and spreads his hands wide. His head is bowed but energy is beginning to pool around him as he calls on his abilities.

"These are not the droids you are looking for." He tells the servants surrounding us in a calm steady tone.

I shoot Brain a hard glare and he answers with a smug smirk, apparently this kid has been raised Star Wars.

I fucking hate Star Wars. A fact that Brain and I have had endless discussions about while on stake out and patrol together. Let me break this down for you, people listen up and hear my words. There are two Sci Fi shows that matter.

Firefly and Star Trek, in that damn order.

The kid hasn't been raised right.

Jedi fucking mind tricks.

Except that it works, but at a cost. I can see the kid wipe away the thin trickle of blood coming out of his nose. If he keeps this up he will stroke out or drop from an aneurism. The servants blink a few times and then drift slowly back to their posts after waving us on.

If any of the other slaves noticed the strangeness of what just happened, they give no sign. They just continue the long slow plod to whatever duties await them in the stadium. They look at nothing, they see nothing, they notice nothing. They have no idea that the HRO is amongst them, hell they likely don't even know that we actually exist.

They have no idea that wolves walk amongst them.

Jones gives me a tiny nod as he shuffles past me, behind him trails a few other familiar faces from the raid on the arsenal the other night. These are Brain's go to people for things like this and I have to trust that he knows his people. I have to trust that he has hand-picked this squad.

He after all was been trained by the best.

We are in.

The rest of the throng goes about their prearranged purposes and we try to look just as deliberate and directed as we go about ours. Pretending to sweep and clean most of our group fans out into the stands stashing a gun here, a grenade there and so forth. Brain and I head down onto the field itself with our little cart of joy. Keela and our son come with us.

His face is grey and tired. I look at him with an ill-defined feeling that I want to somehow ease the burdens he carries. Poor little guy should be doing little league baseball, the Boy Scouts and so on, anything but this. But this is the hand he has been dealt and he is playing like a fucking boss.

Like my old mentor was fond of saying.

Opportunity knocks but trouble just kicks the damn door in.

We wheel the cart down onto the field only having to stop once to mindfuck the traitor guarding the field. Together we manage to get to centerfield and that is where we start to go about the business of planting the bomb. Brain works quickly and efficiently and has the damn thing armed and activated in a few minutes. He sets the timer and that is our signal to disperse and spread ourselves into the group of slaves and start really doing the work that they do.

There aren't enough of us, it is just a plain fact, but we would never have gotten a bigger group through all of the check points we had to pass. We and the weapons we have brought with us will have to serve. Jones takes the group and begins to work them into positions having access to the weapons we have planted. We all have timers on our belts linked to the vampire nuke. Ours are set to give us a ten second warning so that we can put on our sun glasses and prepare for the UV burst and draw our weapons.

Brain says the words and casts a generic concealment spell around the bomb and the kid tells us he is projecting subtle waves of disinterest into the minds of those around us. Nobody will be able to quite care enough to notice the cart sitting on the field.

Now all we have to do is stand pat and wait for darkfall.

Wait for all of the most powerful elder vamps in the city to awaken and gather all in one place with all of their servants and adepts to protect them. Wait for the damn stadium to be bursting with vampire energies that we brought nine people to somehow defeat. It is a hell of a plan.

What could possibly go wrong?

CHAPTER SIXTEEN

I still bear enough of my vampire taint to be able to track almost to the minute the passage of the sun across the sky. Darkfall is coming and it is coming fast.

And so are the vampires.

House by house they come filing in, some alone, some with their entourages. They arrive by some complex protocol that we lowly humans would probably never be able to understand. The Elders of course claim the prime seating and the pecking order ranging up from them into the nose bleed sections.

I keep my head down like a good little slave.

This is by far the most vampires I have ever been close to and the weight of them threatens to pull me under in a dark relentless tide. My marks burn like I have never felt them burn before. So many old vampires in one place, I comfort myself with the knowledge that very soon now, there will be a lot less of them.

It is the little things that count.

Still no sign of any Dark Adepts, they must still be trying to contain the blood camp riots our agents have staged. The longer they stay gone the better for us, they are much harder to deal with than the human servants. The sheer arrogance of the vampires serves to protect us somewhat, for a decade now humans have been blood bags under their heel. The HRO has been a minor irritation at best and they are incapable of imagining that we would have the means and the gall to hit them like this. Every Elder vamp gathered in one place just begs for a bloody ambush but they cannot see us as a serious threat. I take comfort in that and in the weight of the weapons I am carrying. I have lessons I want to teach these fanged fucks before this night is over and there is one main one.

Pay back is a bitch motherfuckers.

The roof of the stadium is open and above I can see stars flickering weakly behind the oily stain that is the barrier the Dark Adepts spelled into place somehow. The barrier my son plans on taking down in some fashion known only to him. The rest of us are charged with keeping him alive and killing enough of these assholes as we can to give him a shot at doing so.

I flick careful glances up at the podium that has been set up by the slaves for the Vampire Council and I recognize a few from my days as a Gun. Can only pray that my new face is enough to fool them and that they don't return the favor. The head of The Council is a light brown skinned man of medium build. He is of course bald as a cue ball and his features sharp edged. He has a naked young woman with long red hair on a leash as his personal blood slave, who squats down next to him with her eyes downcast and trembling slightly in the chill of the night. One of his long fingered hands strokes her hair absently.

Or maybe trembling with hopeless terror.

Even from here I can see that she is covered with scratches, bruises and bite marks. The new head of The Council apparently likes to play with his food.

It was a matter of some debate during our planning sessions but in the end we decided to hit them during his opening speech. My son had wanted to let them get comfortable and caught up in the night's entertainment before setting off the nuke. Brain and the rest of us were not going to watch the humans, being held in holding pens beneath the stadium, be slaughtered for this sick fucks jollies, if we could help it. The kid pressed it, but in the end Brain stared him down and told him flatly that it wasn't going to happen.

A gong sounds nine times in a slow measured beat and the stadium goes very still and quiet.

Almost show time.

The Master vampire head of The Council raises his hands to the sky and turns in a slow circle surveying the gathering of vamps all around him. When he speaks he needs no microphone, his other worldly voice fills the stadium to the point where us poor humans can do nothing but cringe against it.

"Brethren! We are gathered once again to celebrate the night that Seattle fell to us, the night we claimed what is ours by birthright and here in this city, if nowhere else in the world, we no longer hide in the shadows. Here in this city we rule and the humans serve us, this is how it is meant to be." His voice thunders.

Going to have to disagree with him on that one.

"Our allies, the gathered covens of the Dark Adepts worked with us to make this come to pass. Even as we sit here this fine evening preparing for the diversions to come, they are working to quell riots at the blood camps caused by a handful of human agitators. Ah, and it would appear that our allies are now returning to us."

Sure enough Dark Adepts, many of them soaked in blood, that is clearly not their own, begin to step out of the shadows and take their places up on the podium. A polite round of applause greets them that they acknowledge with slight bows. The Grand Coven Master, a small powerfully built clean shaven Hispanic man takes his place next to the Master Vampire.

He whispers something to the leader of The Vampire Council and frowning the vamp leans down to hear it better.

I don't have a good feeling about this.

The Master vamp straightens and raises his hands for silence again and instantly the crowd obeys and the stadium is absolutely silent. All of the dayslaves stand frozen in position awaiting with the docile servitude, which has literally been beaten into them, whatever horror is to come next.

"I regret to inform you my brethren, that we have a traitor in our midst. One who has rejected the dark gift bestowed upon her unworthy being and chosen to betray us to aid the silly little human resistance in their pathetic efforts against us. This cannot stand unpunished, an example must be made. A clear message must be sent to those who would stand against us. The cost of such betrayal is pain beyond reckoning and then the true, final death."

A roar fills the stadium that drives all the humans still standing to their knees, even a few of the newer human servants struggle to remain standing.

I really don't like where this is going.

I glance around me to find my team, things are going to get interesting very soon now. Keela and our boy are to my left, Jones and his crew are scattered in a loose ring about halfway up the bleachers. I can't find Brain at first, but then I see him kneeling with a small group of dayslaves, just to the right of the main podium.

Shit is about to get real sports fans.

Two burly Dark Adepts drag Andrea up to the podium, she is struggling weakly against them but in her starvling state she is no match. Her hands are bound at the wrist with silver chains that must be burning like hell. The Master Vampire slaps her so hard, that for a moment I thought that he must have killed her outright.

But no, she is hauled back to her feet to face him and to give her credit she spits blood into his face.

Then the timer goes off on my wrist.

There is an old saying about how most battle plans fall apart within seconds of the fight really starting.

Yeah, this is like that.

Brain lost his wife to the vampires and it very nearly killed him. The Order recruited him and gave him new purpose serving in the fight against the vampire menace. I gave him the gift of vengeance against the vampire that butchered the love of his life and started him down the path to becoming a Gun. Later he met and fell in love with a bar owner named Jenny, she couldn't handle the world he had come to inhabit and they had ended the relationship. He told me yesterday that she had died in a blood camp because he, despite his desperate best effort, had failed to get her to safety in time.

As I watch the rage that has always been in him boil over, as I watch the weight of all the shit that has happened to him over the years reaches a final breaking point, as I watch I see him decide that he is unable to watch one more person he loves die. As I watch he stands up screaming incoherently and begins firing a sawed off shotgun into the vamps standing in the way between him and Andrea.

Ten seconds doesn't seem like a very long time until guns are firing and people are screaming. Ten seconds doesn't seem like a long time until people are dying all around you.

Then it seems like a fucking eternity.

I say the damn words Twilla whispered into my ear so I can at least die on my feet with my own face on.

CHAPTER SEVENTEEN

Brain fires the shotgun until it is empty and then draws an Uzi full of blessed bullets and carves himself a path to his love. The boldness of the act buys him the few seconds that he needs to reach her and dive on top of her covering her slight form with his own body. The vampires, human servants and Dark Adepts stand there stunned for a moment unable to process what is going on.

Cursing I slip on my sunglasses and pull my Hi-Point out. A Dark Adept forms a curse to throw at my friend and I blow his damn head off before he can finish it. Keela draws her gun and shoots the vampire closest to her in the head three times, in the distance I can hear Jones and his boys opening up.

Fuck me gently with a chainsaw, so much for the damn plan.

My son stands absolutely still with his eyes closed, he is shaking with the power that is roaring through him as he tries to ride out visons burning in his brain, because I am sure this cluster fuck has changed everything. A snarling vamp comes running at him moving so fast that I know I will not be able to shoot it in time.

The boy twitches and the vamp is flung a couple of dozen feet away to slam into a concrete wall. It gets up again and he twitches again and the thing falls to the ground with every single bone in its body shattered.

The vamp does not get up again.

There is a whisper of power and the levitation spell kicks in and the vampire nuke rises slowly into the air. More than one set of eyes follows it as it ascends, wondering what the hell it is.

Duck and cover boys and girls.

There is no explosion, no earth shattering roar, no hot wave of blast carrying shrapnel. No, it goes off like a slow motion flashbulb.

There aren't any fucking words for what happens next.

In that one instant every exposed vampire in the stadium bursts into flame, their screams an awful ear shattering wail of pain and disbelief. They die by the dozens and their human servants' fall writhing on the floor to die with them. The Dark Adepts remain unaffected but they are getting riddled with bullets by our crew and die along with the rest.

The air becomes foul with the ashes of dead vamps and the stench of it is almost too much too bear. I shoot whatever I come across trying to make it over to where Brain has Andrea protected from the pulse. Screaming vampires on fire block my path and I shoot and kick them out of my damn way as I go.

Jones manages to drop a phosphorus grenade from a balcony seat right onto The Master Vampire, who despite being on fire, is still screaming at his entourage to kill all of the humans. The grenade finishes him in a blinding white flash.

I like Jones.

I suddenly feel myself growing a little weaker, a little dizzy. I realize that in the last few seconds I have lost three of my marks as I kill my way towards my friend. I guess we are going to find out what happens when I lose my last marks.

No time to think about that now, as I wade through a hell of dead and dying vampires, human servants, Dark Adepts and sadly plain old humans. The sound of screaming vamps and gunfire blends together in a hellish symphony. The ashes of the dead vamps fall like a grim snow. The percussion line is the steady thump of grenades going off. The pulse from the nuke ends but the bloody damage is done. Even if we fail to drop the barrier we have done cataclysmic damage to the vampires. Their ruling council lies in ashes, their human servants dead with them and Jones and friends are busy slaughtering all of the Dark Adepts they have time and bullets for. It is an awful scene and it is hard to imagine how it could get worse.

Ask a stupid question.

Brain looks at me and a crooked grin flashes across his face and for a moment he looks like my old friend, the boyish screw up I trained into a legendary level Gun. His looks tells me that he finally saved someone, finally in the midst of all this death, he actually saved someone. The look is equal amounts surprise and gratitude.

And then he explodes into a fountain of blood and gore that splatters the surrounding walls and Dark Molly erupts through what remains of him.

"Get the fuck off of me!" She screams as she effortlessly breaks free of the silver chains binding her. The links explode from her and lodge themselves in the screaming flesh of everyone near her. Her scream shatters glass in every direction and even the dying that surround her cringe before it. She stands covered in blood looking wildly in all directions until her eyes settle on me.

She travels the distance between us in less than a blink of an eye and then she is holding me over her head and giving me a vicious shake.

"What the fuck is going on Black Irish?!" She bellows.

I can barely breathe, she is holding me effortlessly over her head by my throat and she is choking the life from me.

"You just killed my friend you fucking bitch." I manage to gasp out with my feet dangling off of the ground.

She glances back and a complicated look flashes across her face. Part regret, part rage, part well, part fuck if I know all the emotions parading across it.

"Shit, that was Brian? Fuck, the other bitch in my head is going to be sooo pissed! Oh well, they loved each other, did you know that? Guess what? True love splatters!" She giggles as she licks the blood of my friend off of her other hand. The pressure on my throat increases and I know that she means to kill me as well.

My tattoo gives a wrenching spasm and Twilla is back in the game. She reforms between me and Dark Molly.

"Get away from him you bitch!" She says as she drives a fist right into the crazy vampire's face.

Dark Molly drops me and then Twilla delivers three bone crushing roundhouse kicks to her head in a row driving her backwards and away from me. Moving with more than human speed she continues to batter at the crazy vamp.

Around us the chaos continues, most of the stadium is burning now and thick black smoke from the burning seats mingles with the ashes of vampires. Badly wounded vampires are crawling around, most of them still on fire. Keela kills two that try for her, desperately needing blood to heal themselves. I have no time to mourn my friend just now, we can't stay here we need to get out. Jones runs by me yelling and sums it all up nicely.

"Everybody get the fuck out, right, fucking, now!"

The soul of a poet that man.

Not going to be that easy of course.

Dark Molly takes a few more hard hits and allows herself to be backed into a corner, I have been in enough fights to know a fake when I see one and I open my mouth to shout a warning to Twilla.

And then the crazy fucking vampire bitch goes and does the motherfucking impossible yet one more time.

She uses magic.

She fucking uses magic.

Jesus wept.

Fuck me gently with a chainsaw.

Dark Molly

CHAPTER EIGHTEEN

My old mentor sold me down the river to a master vampire named Martin who along with his human servant Jeremy sought to follow a dark ritual that if successful would have turned me into a new kind of vampire. To overcome a limitation that the vampires had long chafe against, the inability of their kind to wield magic of any kind. The ritual sought to make me into a more deadly type of vampire.

A vampire that could wield magic.

The ritual was interrupted when The Order's special branch called The Intervention…well intervened I would suppose is as good of way of saying as any.

But it would appear that someone else has succeeded where the sick fucks who tried to turn me failed.

Dark Molly traps Twilla in a binding spell that drops the imp on her knees before her, helpless and defenseless. Then with a wicked grin Dark Molly sketches the rune of banishment in the space between them and with one last horrible scream Twilla vanishes in a burst of brimstone and flame.

Sent back to where the imp came from.

Oh no she didn't!

A spasm of pain in my borrowed eye tells me that the old man isn't happy with this latest development, neither am I.

I am done with this. Drawing a Mac Ten from beneath my coveralls I walk towards her spraying blessed bullets as I come. Keela takes my cue and starts firing her 9mm at her from another direction.

The vampire jerks from the impact of all those bullets like a marionette in the hands of a Parkinson's patient.

She goes down but she doesn't stay down. Struggling to her feet she turns towards us just long enough to give us the finger and then she is gone in a burst of vampire speed.

I stare in the general direction that she blurred away in. What the hell was she? Every damn thing about her was flat out impossible. Her dual nature, her strength and power and above all bloody else, her ability to work magic.

No time for the mystery of her right now. Way past time to get the hell out of Dodge. The air is so thick with smoke and ash that it is going to be a painful game of blind man's bluff just making it out to the street.

Keela and I put our son between us and try to follow Jones and his boys through the hell we created trying not to choke on the noxious fumes. I shoot a twitching human servant in the head as I pass, it is more kindness than the traitorous prick deserves.

A dazed looking vamp confronts us and I empty most of a clip into his bald head, which explodes quite nicely and his carcass falls out of our way. A Dark Adept crawls up to me, clearly dying from multiple gunshot wounds and I give the little bastard a mercy bullet as well.

I toss the empty Mac Ten aside and draw my Hi-Point and my Snake Slayer Derringer. Carrying one in each hand, I keep on moving through the smoke and ash trying to keep a visual on Keela and our son.

Other humans begin to run past us, apparently the humans kept in the holding pens have taken advantage of the chaos and made good their own escape. They are a starved, filthy, desperate looking lot and they don't even look at us as they run as fast as their weakened bodies can go by. A man holding hands with a woman is the only one who even glances at us and as he does something passes between us.

I know him.

Well not really, don't know his name or anything but a lifetime ago or so, before I took my little stroll into the shadows, he had been a rookie cop who had the bad luck to run into Brain and I when we were in no mood to be fucked with. We were on our way to try and rescue Keela from an insane master vamp and just didn't have time for a chat just then.

So I had knocked him out.

My bad.

Unlike most of the fleeing slaves he had stopped to pick up a gun, a short barreled tactical pump action shotgun. He must have taken it off of a guard because we sure didn't bring anything like that with us. The years have not been good to him, but I have always been good with faces and I know that it is him.

The look he gives me tells me he knows that it is me as well.

He raises the shotgun with an empty expression on his dirty face and fires.

Taking out the Dark Adept who just stepped out of a shadow behind me and to my left.

Giving me a small nod he hustles the woman away and in seconds they are lost to me in the billowing clouds of smoke and ash.

After what seems like a few eternities, I stumbled out of the stadium and out onto the street. Coughing my damn lungs out, I lean against a bad piece of public art and try to focus on my surroundings.

Out of the damn fire pan and into the fire.

CHAPTER NINETEEN

We emerge into the middle of an out and out street brawl. Vampires attacking humans, Dark Adepts being assaulted by humans and the reverse of that. Jones and pals spraying any likely target with blessed lead and a panicked mob of freed slaves spilling through all this. No less chaotic than the scene inside had been but at least we can see our targets and breathe the air.

For right now we will call that a win.

Behind us the stadium is fully engulfed in fire, and smoke continues to pour from it steadily. Everything inside of it now is dead. My old friend is getting a Vikings funeral and I think that he would have approved.

Rest in peace brother.

Two vampires come at me from the low lying roof of a nearby building, my marks burn hot because they are both over a hundred years old. Both of them must have been outside the stadium when the nuke went off because they are unscathed and very pissed off. Keela puts a whole clip into the head of one of them on the fly and he smashes to the ground as dead meat.

She wasn't this good before I left, somebody has been practicing.

The other gets a 410 blessed slug in the chest and a load of blessed buckshot to the face from the Snake Slayer and he goes down.

A double tap from the Hi-Point and he goes out.

That is when vampire number three appears out of nowhere and grabs my son.

A bubble surrounds us now, all I can see is the vampire cruelly twisting my son's arm as the foul thing tries to drag him away. Tunnel vison blocks off everything happening around me and the shots from my 9mm sound like distant firecrackers as I put six rounds into the vamp before I run empty.

Jones appears and puts a few rounds into the vamps back, not terribly sporting but effective as the vampire falls down and releases my son, who runs over to stand by his mother.

The vamp smiles wickedly and wills his hands into exploding razor sharp claws. Moving with speed no human could hope to dodge he rakes those claws across Jones' belly, he falls to the ground suddenly consumed with the task of holding his guts inside his body with blood drenched hands.

I reload with my last magazine and walk towards the bastard and I give him all eight rounds into his damned skull. My slide locks back and a couple of things happen at once.

First the fucking vampire dies.

Then the last of my marks flickers out.

Ruh Roh…

I fall to my knees against the hard cold ground. All strength has left me and I fall a new born kitten weak to the ground. Between one breath and the next I feel the vampire taint that I have carried finally leave me. It has granted me strength and speed that has allowed me to carry out my form of justice against killer vamps but I am not sorrowed at its loss. It is a burden I have long carried and I have now earned the right to set it down.

Thirteen marks, one for each of the human victims I served up to my vampire Master. The Order performed an archaic ritual on me to give me this chance to redeem myself. I have now followed the letter of that ritual and killed thirteen killer vampires. Debt now…. paid in full. The idea at the time was that the loss of my final mark would kill me and send me to the judgment of a higher power.

Brain, one of the single most brilliant men I have ever met, had put forth the theory. The change wrought in me by the aborted dark ritual canceled the death sentence of losing my last mark, but there really had been no way to test the theory until now.

Suddenly Keela and our son are by my side holding me in a more or less upright sitting position.

"I am truly sorry Father, my visions told me that it would take the blood of the redeemed to end the spell that created the dark barrier. Forgive me but it wasn't until you touched me that I knew you were destined to be the redeemed as soon as you lost the last of your marks." He tells me and there are tears running down his face.

Keela gives him a sharp look and then starts crying herself. Her hand all but crushes mine, she is holding it so tight.

My son stands above me now and a nimbus of power begins to swirl around him, he withdraws into a distant place inside of himself and gives himself over to the visions that led us all here. The flicker of power around us seems to separate us from the rest of the night somehow.

The tears are gone and his face is blank, his eyes closed as he follows possibilities and threads of power through some haunted inner landscape. When he speaks his voice seems to echo oddly around us.

"The blood of the redeemed shall run with the ashes of the dark defeated and as it runs it will wash away the ruin of the city and that which was stained, shall then be cleansed."

A thought crosses my mind, I feel like I am more likely than not dying, but I am not actually bleeding.

The boy's eyes fly open and he walks stiffly over and squats down next to me and dips his finger into the ash settling like snow on the street. He then draws a glyph of some kind on my forehead. The glyph tingles strangely and then goes ice cold. Then gently but firmly he pulls my gun out of my hands and stands up again.

Oh, this is going to suck.

"I am the focus so I must not intervene directly, another force must do that which is required."

He hands the gun to Keela with a deep sigh and starts to retreat back into himself again, but before he does he gives her an order.

"Shoot him mother."

My son just ordered his mother to shoot his father, I am pretty sure that Hallmark doesn't make a card for that.

Hallmark continues to fail me.

More emotions than can be counted flash across my girls face as she holds the gun in her hands. Her hands hold the gun like she has been trained to, but they do tremble.

"Joe...." She begins in a small voice not looking at me, she has let go of my hand now.

"Do it." I tell her flatly. If it will bring the spell down so be it. Like I have said my life was pledged to atone for my sins and protect this city. I have now succeeded at the first and I will give my life for the second.

My borrowed eye twinges and I decide to cheat the old fuck out of his grand finale, I reach into my pocket and slowly take out the eye patch and put the damn thing on. Let the old bastard find an old Lifetime movie to watch, the end times of Joe Gunn has been canceled for your viewing pleasure. It is a small victory, but for right now we will call it a win.

My girl loves me, I know that like I know that I am right handed. It is a fact, it is a given. I also know that she is a soldier in the same cause I have fought for so long. The same cause that Brain just died for. The same cause they spent long hard years fighting while I slept in the shadows. She glances up at the oily stain polluting the night sky above us and looks around at the humans and vampires killing each other all around us.

"Hurry." Our son says urgently and for a moment I can feel it with him. I can feel the fates of everyone around us balanced on knives edge. Our window of opportunity is closing fast.

Staring down at me she flicks off the safety. She might be able to do this but she will forever bear the weight of it. I close my eyes and wish there was a way to spare her of the burden of it.

A gun goes off twice and two bullets slam into my chest laying me flat out on the hard cold ground. My eyes open and I see Keela looking confused.

"I wanted to spare her the burden of it." Jones says weakly lowering the gun he can barely hold. He gives me a small nod and then he dies.

Thank you brother.

"And the blood of the kind will tip the balance. What was done will now come undone." The boy's voice now holds a note of triumph in it.

He throws his hands upward in a sharp casting gesture and all the power that had been thrumming in him is released into the night.

For a long horrible moment, nothing happens.

For that long horrible moment failure at unspeakable costs stares us all in the face and laughs a jackal's laugh at us.

Then the oily stain that writhed in the night sky for over a decade flickers once and then simply vanishes.

If I know my Order, teams of Guns are already flooding into the city from every possible direction. They will liberate the blood camps and wipe out every single damn vamp that survived this night's carnage. They will provide aid and comfort for all the human survivors and as much as possible redeem themselves by saving what is left of this city. Whatever comes of the vampire becoming public knowledge will come, but for now they will save everyone that they can and kill every vampire that had any damn thing to do with this horror show.

So much blood, my hands instinctively try to cover the wounds but I am bleeding out. My hands are slick with blood. My vision is already starting to blur and dim.

My son gently takes one hand and Keela sobs and takes the other. A thought whispers faintly in a back corner of my mind. It slowly works it ways to my voice.

"You said you would tell me what your name means." I manage to gasp wetly as I lie there.

"Tumaini, Father, it is a Swahili word." He whispers softly and his voice is just a boy's voice now. All power has fled back into whatever corner of his being he keeps it.

I stare up at the now clear and untainted sky and with my girl and my son holding me I take my last few breaths.

"It means hope, Father. It means hope….." His voice is tired and broken by his starting to sob.

Fair enough. My eyes close and I let my last breath rattle out of my body.

I haven't failed my city, there is now hope to be had.

We will call that a win.

The End

So we come to the end of the Joe Gunn saga. Yes, boys and girls this is the end, he really is dead and gone. A huge thank you goes out to all of you who have hung in there through all four books. We are humbly grateful for the fans we met at events and conventions and for everyone out there who has downloaded an eBook or ordered a paperback. The author would like to thank his long suffering wife and Editor Gail Anderson for her tireless dedication to the cause. He would also like to thank his fearless and fearsome cosplayers Chris Harris and Andrea

Adamick for bringing the characters to life. Of course the usual thank you to The Pickled Onion Pub in the Renton Highlands for providing me a fun environment with lots of cold beer to lubricate the creative process. "Mind your pints" everyone. This series has ended but stayed tuned because we here at Alucard Press have more tricks up our sleeves…

THE BLACK IRISH CHRONICLES

BLACK IRISH-BOOK ONE

IRISH LULLABY-BOOK TWO

IRISH CAR BOMB-BOOK THREE

IN THE COUNTRY OF THE BLIND

(A STAND ALONE JOE GUNN NOVEL)

Alucard Press-All rights reserved

Made in the USA
San Bernardino, CA
08 May 2016